ANNIE'S ATTIC MYSTERIES®

Letters
in the Attic

DeAnna Julie Dodson

Annie's®

AnniesFiction.com

Library of Congress-in-Publication Data
Letters in the Attic / by DeAnna Julie Dodson
p. cm.
I. Title
              2009911073

AnniesFiction.com
(800) 282-6643
Annie's Attic Mysteries®
Series Editors: Janice Tate and Ken Tate
Series Creator: Stenhouse & Associates, Ridgefield, Connecticut

10 11 12 13 14 | Printed in China | 9

~ 1 ~

Annie Dawson stood on the front porch of Grey Gables, forgetting for the moment that she carried a bag of groceries in each arm. The light dusting of early-October snow had melted, and now the day was crisp and clear, the brilliant reds and yellows of the maple trees and the rich green of the white pines vibrant against the aqua sky. Maybe these were exactly the colors she needed for her next crochet project—the colors of Maine in autumn.

The ladies at the Hook and Needle Club had told her weeks ago that she ought to make herself a nice sweater for the cool weather to come.

"Maine's not like Texas where it stays hot until November sometimes," Mary Beth had told her.

Annie smiled to think of that now. Just yesterday her daughter, LeeAnn, had mentioned that the temperature was up to 85 degrees in Dallas. But a few weeks ago, back when Mary Beth had made her comment, Annie hadn't decided if she would still be in Stony Point when the cold weather came, or if she would even need a sweater warm enough for a chilly fall evening in Maine. Now it was October, and she still hadn't really decided. But she hadn't left, either.

There was too much yet to be done at Grey Gables. Gram had left her the old house and an attic full of memories and mysteries, too, treasured handwork and precious remembrances from a long life well and thoroughly lived. Having those things properly cared for, seeing them sold or given to those who would truly appreciate them, was a task Gram had entrusted to Annie. As much as she missed her daughter and her twin grandchildren, Annie couldn't go back to Texas quite yet.

She had to admit, too, that she was enjoying the changing seasons. When she was young, she had visited Gram in the summers. She hadn't been in Stony Point during harvesttime, and hadn't seen the changing of the leaves or the coming of the snow. Maybe people who lived up north thought the snow was a nuisance. In her part of Texas, it was a brief and beautiful thing. What would it be like to live in a place where, every winter, it came to stay?

Annie took one last deep breath of the brisk air before going into the house. She headed straight for the kitchen, where she set down the groceries. It was well past noon, and Boots would be clamoring to be fed. Usually she was meowing and rubbing against Annie's ankles the minute she came home.

"Boots? Here, kitty, kitty. Lunchtime."

Returning to the entryway, Annie picked up the mail that had been slipped through the slot in the front door and put it on the little table alongside her purse. Back in the kitchen, she poured a bowlful of crunchies. The smell of the dry cat food and the sound of it jingling against the porcelain bowl ought to bring Miss Boots running.

"Come eat, Boots."

Annie helped herself to a banana from the kitchen counter and then checked her answering machine: three messages.

"Mrs. Dawson, this is Josephine Booth from the library.

We received the book you requested and will hold it for you until next Friday. Please stop by at your convenience to pick it up, or let us know if you're no longer interested in checking it out. Thank you. We hope to see you soon."

Lovely. She couldn't wait to dive into the book on restoring old homes that one of Alice's Divine Décor friends had recommended, and she really wanted to see what else the library had to offer on the subject.

"Mom? I forgot to tell you about the party we're having for Herb's birthday next month, just in case you want to … oh, I don't know … come home for it? Call me."

Annie shook her head. LeeAnn wasn't always subtle with her hints about Annie coming back to Texas.

"Hello, Annie. This is Clara Robbins. Just wanted to let you know we're planning a harvest banquet at the church, and any ideas you'd like to contribute would be very much welcome. Be thinking about it, and I'll let you know as soon as we have a time set for the planning meeting. Call me if you have questions."

Annie made a mental note to offer to make some of Gram's unparalleled berry pies for the occasion. Other than that, she'd volunteer to help however she was able. And she'd see what Alice, her friend since childhood and now her next-door neighbor, had in mind. It would be fun and not a bad way to get better acquainted with more of her neighbors in Stony Point.

She took another bite of the banana and went through the mail. Bills mostly, except for one oversized envelope addressed in a large, careful scrawl to "Grammy." Smiling, Annie opened it and found two folded sheets of manila paper. One was a drawing of a princess with floor-length yellow curls, a bright pink gown, a tiara, and a sparkling magic wand. It was inscribed "From Joanna." The other was unsigned, but it had to be from her twin, John. It was a Technicolor dinosaur breathing flames from its nostrils at something that looked like an astronaut. Yes, it was definitely from John.

Smiling still, Annie took both pictures and added them to the gallery on her refrigerator. She glanced at the cat's bowl and noticed the food was still untouched. Where could that rascal be?

She finished the last bite of banana, dropped the peel into the trash, and went into the living room. There was no little fur ball curled up on the couch.

"Boots, come eat!"

Annie looked in a few of Boots' favorite places—the sunny window in the dining room, the overstuffed chair in the library, even under the afghan puddled on the living room couch. No Boots. Finally out of options, Annie went upstairs. A quick look around told her that the attic door was open just wide enough to allow the passage of a lithe little gray body. She'd have to be more careful about closing that door all the way. Nothing intrigued a cat more than someplace she wasn't allowed.

Annie pushed open the door and went up the stairs. "Boots? Are you in here? Boots?"

She heard a sound—half purr, half sleepy meow—and a little gray head popped up out of a partially open drawer.

"That is not your bed, missy." Annie marched over to the antique bird's-eye maple dresser at one side of the attic, pretending to scold as she picked up the cat. "Bad enough you think the whole house is your playroom. You don't need to be up here getting into Gram's things."

Boots purred and butted her head against Annie's hand, begging to be scratched, and Annie obliged. "All right, flatterer, you're forgiven. Now what were you sleeping on?"

Annie looked in the drawer and shook her head.

"Those are Gram's hand-embroidered dish towels, you know." She set the cat on the floor so she could open the drawer a little more and then caught her breath before an involuntary little shriek could escape her. Then she laughed. OK, so it wasn't a real severed hand, just an old rubber one from some forgotten Halloween. Why in the world had Gram kept the silly thing, and what else was in the drawer?

Annie rummaged around a little more. A couple of Victorian-looking Christmas ornaments, some seed packets, two decks of playing cards rubber-banded together, and shoved toward the back was a packet of envelopes tied with a piece of yarn. Annie remembered that yarn. It was the variegated green she had used on one of her very first afghans Gram had taught her to make when she was a girl. She didn't even try to think how many years ago that had been.

Boots rubbed against her ankles, demanding to be fed.

"Oh, so *now* you're hungry. Well, go on."

Annie picked up the letters and shooed Boots down the stairs and out of the attic, careful to close the door all the way behind her. As she made her way down to the living room, Annie felt her smile grow wider. The envelopes were a bit faded now, but as she flipped through them, she remembered the brightly colored inks and the exuberant curvy letters, complete with red and pink hearts to dot every letter "i." She remembered the little smiley faces and rainbows that had been so popular when she was just out of grade school.

She remembered Susan.

Annie was fourteen that year, and she and her Stony Point friends were building a sand castle—a sand castle that was meant to be the biggest and best ever. She couldn't help noticing the skinny girl with white-blond hair who stood at the edge of the grass watching, though she didn't invite her to help with the building. But Gram had noticed the girl too.

She waved Annie over to the bench where she was reading. "That little girl looks about your age, honey. I bet she'd love to help you with your sand castle."

Gram never liked to see anyone left out, and young Annie felt kind of sorry for the girl, so she went over to her.

"Hi. What's your name?" The blond girl smiled, looking shyly at the ground. "I'm Susan Morris. I'm a good swimmer."

"I'm Annie. I like to swim too. You want to work on our sand castle? My grandma said you might want to."

Susan shrugged. "Guess so, if it's OK."

"Sure. Come on." Annie took her to the rest of her friends. "This is Susan. She can help us."

Soon Susan lost most of her shyness and seemed to be enjoying herself, even though Alice had assigned to her the task of hauling wet sand from near the surf. By the time the magnificent, or at least large, sand castle was built, Susan and Annie had found they had something in common. Annie visited Maine only in the summer. Susan lived in a house outside Stony Point and didn't know many of the town kids. In a way, they were both outsiders.

Gram smiled consent when Annie asked if Susan could

come back to Grey Gables with them for lunch. At the house, Annie showed her new friend her first attempts at crochet, the start of the variegated green afghan, and Gram offered to teach Susan how to make one too.

That was the first summer the two girls spent together. In late August, Annie had returned to Texas and school, so she and Susan had exchanged letters—*these* letters. Or at least these were the letters Susan had written to her.

Annie opened one at random. How it took her back. She was fourteen again, and everything was so important.

I got an A+ on my history test. I couldn't remember which president was Old Hickory, but I must have guessed right ... My mom got me some new tap shoes, and I'm taking lessons in Brunswick now. Mom says I needed a better teacher than Mrs. Herttenberger if I'm going to be a real dancer someday ... Billy Kinneman sits behind me in science this year ...

Laughing softly, Annie returned the letter to its envelope and chose another. More smileys and rainbows and hearts.

Daddy got me my own telephone for my birthday. I wish it wasn't long distance to call you. Why do you have to live in Texas anyway? ... Bobby Marchment tried to sit by me on the bus to the planetarium, but Billy made him move ... Bunny had four puppies last night ...

One more, Annie promised herself, and then she absolutely had to get some housework done. She chose one toward the bottom of the stack, postmarked May 1980.

ANNIE!!!!!! You won't believe it! I'm going to live in New York! I didn't tell you because I was afraid I wouldn't be chosen, but I auditioned for a dance program there and was accepted! Mom and Dad didn't think they could afford it, but I'm getting a scholarship and everything! My Aunt Kim lives there, and I'm going to get to stay with her! Isn't it cool!!!!

Annie shook her head and laughed again. All those exclamation points. How excited Susan had been, and Annie had been almost as excited for her. It must have been a busy time for her, too, because there weren't many letters after that, and Susan hadn't come back to Stony Point the next few summers. Annie had lost track of her. Her marriage to Wayne, college, and helping him manage their Chevrolet dealership had kept her close to home in Texas. Gram had to come visit her there instead of Annie coming to Grey Gables. But what had become of Susan?

Annie sighed. Could it be thirty years ago already? It seemed incredible, but the time had passed in the blink of an eye. Did Susan ever become a "real" dancer and perform on Broadway as she had so often dreamed? Perhaps her days on the stage were over, and now she was the one teaching young hopefuls. Maybe her hair, like Annie's, was showing some silver in the gold. Had she kept in touch with Billy Kinneman, or was someone else the love of her life? Did she have children? Grandchildren? Maybe she, too, was widowed.

Somebody in Stony Point had to have kept up with Susan. Wouldn't it be great to see her again?

Annie tapped the stack of letters against the edge of the

coffee table, thinking. Mary Beth knew everything about everybody. Too bad the needlework club didn't meet until Tuesday. The meeting would have given her the perfect opportunity to ask about Susan. Of course, if she were to start on a new sweater, she'd need some more yarn. A perfect excuse to visit A Stitch in Time for supplies and a little information too.

She could always call Alice. Alice had been in Stony Point all her life, and she knew almost as much about everybody as Mary Beth did.

Annie reached for the telephone, but jumped with surprise when it chose that moment to start ringing.

"Hello?"

"Annie? How'd you know I was on the line? It didn't even ring."

"Alice!" Annie laughed. "Well, it rang here. Startled me! And you must have read my mind or something. I was just about to call you."

"Oh yeah? I bet it's about the harvest banquet thing at the church. I got a message from Clara about it."

"Yeah, me too. Of course, I may be back in Texas by the time they have the banquet."

Alice snorted. "Don't be silly. You can't go back yet. You haven't gone through even half of the stuff your grandmother left up in that attic."

"Tell me about it. In fact, that's what I was going to call you about just now. Boots got up into the attic, and she was sleeping right on top of some old letters from when I was in junior high."

"Ooooh, from an old boyfriend?"

Annie chuckled. "Don't be silly. I was only thirteen or so."

"Don't *you* be silly. You know you had a crush on that boy who played the drums one summer. What was his name?"

"The drums?" Annie thought for a moment and then laughed. "Dan. Dan Foster. Oh, and he never even talked to me."

"And you cried and cried when you had to go home that year."

"I did," Annie admitted, giggling. "And the next year I couldn't stand him."

Alice laughed too. "So if it's not love letters, what did you find?"

"Come over and have some coffee, and I'll show you."

"It had better be something good for me to come all the way over there."

"Alice! You live next door."

Alice laughed again. "All right. All right. I'll be right over."

Annie hung up the phone and went to open the front door. Alice was already making her way across the autumn-brown grass from the carriage house next to Grey Gables. She waved as Annie came out onto the porch.

Annie waved back. "Look at you. That's a great jacket."

"You like it?" Alice's eyes sparkled as she modeled her quilted jacket and pleated slacks in blue silk. "Notice anything else?"

She came up the steps and stopped to let Annie look her over.

"That's a new necklace, isn't it?"

Alice nodded and then turned her head to one side and then to the other. "Earrings too."

The necklace and earrings were sapphires set in reddish gold, delicate and tasteful, an ideal complement to Alice's blue eyes and auburn hair.

"Very nice. Is that the new line?"

"Just picked up the samples today, and I have a big Princessa jewelry party scheduled for next Tuesday afternoon. What do you think?"

Annie opened the front door, and they both went inside.

"I think you'll sell a ton of those, but they'll never look as perfect on anyone else."

Alice laughed and shook her head. "You're such a flatterer. Now what's this amazing find you were going to show me?"

"Do you remember Susan Morris?"

"Susan Morris." Alice was silent for a minute. "The name sounds familiar. Susan Morris. Susan Morris. Oh, of course. She moved to New York ages ago, didn't she?"

"She was going to be a dancer and went to live with her aunt so she could go to some fancy school there, remember?" Annie showed Alice the packet of letters. "We used to write each other during the school year. I haven't thought about her in years."

Alice picked up one of the envelopes. "Yeah, I remember her now. Her family had that house off the far west end of Elm Street. But if she wrote to you while you were in Texas, how'd these end up here?"

"I brought them back with me one summer. It was a year or so after Susan moved to New York. She'd written me that she was planning to be in Stony Point again, and I thought it would be fun for us to look at the letters we wrote when we were 'little kids.' We were all grown up then and beyond that kind of silliness. Guess I never got back home with them, and of course Gram would never throw anything out."

"And that was when?"

"About the time I turned 15."

Alice shook her head. "Practically ready for the old folks' home by then, huh?"

Annie laughed. "You want some coffee?"

"That'd be great."

The two women went into the kitchen. Alice sat at the big kitchen table while Annie filled the coffeepot.

"You and Susan must have had a good time looking at those letters," Alice said.

"Actually, she didn't end up coming after all. She had a chance to be in a dance troupe that summer and didn't make it back to Maine. I never saw her again, and we pretty much lost touch after that."

"Yeah, I know how that can be. I bet she did all right as a dancer, tall and slim and pretty as she was. I remember wishing I had long blond curls like hers. She came back, you know. To Stony Point."

"She did?"

"I'm pretty sure she did. Couldn't tell you exactly when—a long time ago—but I did hear she was back. I never really kept up with her, though. John and I had our troubles, and then the divorce, and everything made it pretty hard for me to mind anyone's business but my own. Susan must have left again sometime. She's not here now, that's for sure."

Annie sighed. "That's too bad. We always had such a good time together. Gram taught us both to crochet."

"Yeah, she was over here all the time."

"Now, don't be jealous. Gram spent plenty of time with you, and when it mattered too."

"She did that." There was a sudden wistfulness in Alice's expression. "I could still use her advice and her shoulder to cry on."

"Me too."

Annie swallowed down a sudden tightness in her throat. Gram hadn't been gone long, and sometimes Annie ached just to hear her voice again. But Gram wouldn't have held with self-pity. Not for a minute.

Annie cleared her throat. "Now what about the banquet? The message I got wasn't very specific."

"Neither was mine," Alice said. "Do you have any ideas?"

"Not really. I thought I could make some of Gram's pies to take, but other than that I don't know. I'll be happy to help however I can, of course, if I'm still here."

"I guess I'll make my usual pumpkin bread. I know Reverend Wallace likes it, but it would be nice to try something new once in a while." Alice's voice brightened. "Maybe we should put our heads together and figure out something fresh and exciting for this year."

Annie frowned. "Are you sure you don't remember anything else about when Susan was here? After she came back from New York, of course."

"I thought we were talking about the banquet." Alice glanced over at the gurgling coffeepot. "And I thought you invited me over for some coffee."

Annie laughed and got the cups.

2

The next morning, Annie parked her burgundy Malibu in front of the stately white-columned Stony Point library and went inside. She stopped for a moment in the foyer, loving the feeling of being surrounded by so many books and promising herself a return visit when she had time to spend the whole morning browsing. Then she went into the Great Room and up to the Circulation Desk.

"Good morning, Grace," she said softly, and the petite woman behind the desk looked up with a smile.

"Well, hello there. Just a sec." Grace turned to the low shelf behind her, found a book tagged *Dawson*, and handed it to Annie. "Is that what you're after?"

"Oooh, pretty." Annie opened the decorating book she had requested and flipped through a few pages. "I already see a couple of things I'd like to try at Grey Gables. Thanks for requesting it for me. I didn't know interlibrary loans were so fast."

Grace winked. "Depends on who you know."

"I guess you know just about everybody in town. Do you remember Susan Morris? She's about my age. Moved to New York maybe about 1980."

"Morris?" Grace drew her dark brows together, thinking. "That's quite a while ago. Was she any relation to the Morrises who lived way out on Elm Street? Ellen and Jack?"

"Those were her parents' names, if I remember right. You don't know where Susan might be now, do you?"

"No. If she's still in Stony Point, she doesn't come to the library. I guess I could see if she has an active card, but I think I'd remember if she checked anything out more than once or twice."

"Would you mind looking?" Grace looked at her a little oddly, so Annie added, "Susan and I were good friends when I used to come here for the summer, but we've lost touch. I'd like to know how she's doing these days."

"All right, let me check for you." Grace tapped a few keys on the computer keyboard. "No Susan Morris in our database. If she had a library card, it was before we computerized in 1985. Do you remember her address?"

Annie tried to picture the envelopes that were still lying on the coffee table in her living room. 214? 216?

"I think it was 214 Elm."

Grace keyed in the address. "Not Morris."

"Could you try 216?"

Grace obliged and then shook her head. "Sorry."

With a sigh, Annie handed Grace her library card. "Well, thanks for trying, anyway. I guess I'll just take my book and be on my way."

Grace scanned the card and the book, and handed them both back to Annie. "If there's something else I can help you with, just come back anytime."

Annie left the book in her car trunk and walked up Main Street. The Cup & Saucer was gearing up for the lunch crowd, so she didn't stop in to talk to Peggy Carson. She'd see her at the next meeting of the Hook and Needle Club.

Instead, she went straight to A Stitch in Time.

"Annie! What are you doing here? I didn't expect to see you until the meeting on Tuesday." Mary Beth came from behind the counter with a smile on her roundish face. "You must have run out of something."

"Actually, I decided I'd like to make myself a nice, thick sweater."

Mary Beth's smile broadened. "So you're staying in Stony Point after all."

"Now, now. Don't jump to conclusions. I'm just making a sweater, not a commitment. How are you stocked for new and delicious crochet patterns?"

"How about we have a look? Do you have anything specific in mind?"

"Just something nice and warm. I'm not sure what I want, but I'll know it when I see it."

Annie and Mary Beth went over to the wall that housed needlework patterns of all kinds. There was a generous section of leaflets and books for crocheted sweaters, and the two women spent several minutes investigating and discussing a variety of them. Mary Beth made a few suggestions, but none of them was quite what Annie wanted. Then she saw it down on the rack nearest the floor.

"Oh, I like this one." Annie brought the pattern book over to the counter to look at it. "What do you think?"

The photograph showed a young woman raking autumn leaves. Her long-sleeved sweater looked as cozy and bright as the hearth fire in an old country kitchen. It would be perfect.

Mary Beth turned the book so she could see it the right way around. "Oh, that's one of my favorites—new and delicious. It'll look great on you too. Not that anything doesn't."

Annie snickered. "You should see me first thing in the morning."

"Ahem." Mary Beth tugged at the sweater that covered her stocky frame. "I just know that not everybody can wear those horizontal stripes. Do you know what colors you want? I have some really nice worsted yarns that would be great for something like this."

"I want something for fall, but bright, you know? I feel like going back to the '70s for some reason."

"Actually, this is a vintage pattern—a '70s reprint."

"I thought so. It's nice and cheerful. Reminds me of those crazy striped kneesocks that had individual toes. Remember those?"

Laughing, Mary Beth took Annie over to the yarn section of the store and started pulling out soft skeins in a range of vibrant colors.

"Oh, yes, these are great." Annie selected the colors that she had seen from her front porch the day before: azure, crimson, gold and pine—the colors of Maine in autumn.

Mary Beth checked the list of materials the pattern required. "You'll need two more colors if you're going to do it the way they show here."

"Hmm." Annie closed her eyes for a moment, remembering; then she selected two more skeins of yarn, burnt orange for the leaves and a darker blue for the sea. "How about these?"

Mary Beth smiled. "Lovely. And you have a size H hook already, right?"

"Oh yes. I've got every size from 00 to 14 and B through S. You don't think Betsy Holden's granddaughter would be without everything she could possibly need for crochet, do you?"

"Of course not. As your grandmother always said, 'The right tool for the right job.' Now, what else can I get for you?"

"Maybe a little information?"

"About what?" Mary Beth's dark eyes sparkled with intrigue as she rang up Annie's purchases. "Or should I say, 'About who?' "

Annie shrugged. "I guess there's a reason I'm thinking about the '70s today. I found a stack of letters from a friend from my junior high days, and I'd like to get back in touch with her."

"Somebody from Stony Point?"

"Susan Morris. Do you remember her?"

"She moved to New York, didn't she? Years ago. Came back here a while later and left again after her parents died, poor thing."

"When was that? Do you remember?"

Mary Beth considered for a moment. "Must have been sometime in the late '80s. She was still pretty young at the time. I thought she—"

The cordless phone on the store counter gave a shrill ring. Mary Beth excused herself and picked it up.

"A Stitch in Time. This is Mary Beth. How can I help you? Yes, Mr. Hodges, I have been trying to reach you. It's about my cabinets … I see. Can you hold just a minute? Thank you."

She put the phone down and turned back to Annie.

"I'm sorry, but I've been trying to get a problem with this guy straightened out for more than a month now. I ordered new storage cabinets for the basement, but they sent the wrong thing. They have our orders and someone else's all mixed up and have been sending us bills for stuff we never got. Do you mind if we chat later? This may take a while, and Kate's not in to help with the store right now."

"No problem," Annie assured her. "We can always talk on Tuesday."

"Thanks."

Mary Beth put the pattern and the yarn into a bag and gave them to Annie; then she returned to the phone.

"Mr. Hodges? Yes, I'm sorry to have kept you waiting. Now, I explained all of this to a Ms. White on the fourteenth of last month, and to a Mr. Carson a week before that, and that was after ..."

Annie gave Mary Beth a cheery wave and left the shop. Mary Beth had her hands full as the owner and manager of A Stitch in Time, even though it was obvious that she loved everything to do with threads and yarns and fabrics. Did she ever take a day off?

Annie was thankful that Wayne had left her well provided for when he passed away. Of course, no amount of security could fill the empty space he had left behind, but at least she didn't have to worry about how she was going to make it financially without him. It was nice to have the freedom to do what she wanted most of the time.

She smiled as she walked back to her car. What she wanted now was to dive into these glorious yarns and get started on her new sweater. It was Friday. Tuesday would be here soon enough, and then she could find out more. Surely, between them all, the members of the Hook and Needle Club could help her figure out how to get back in touch with Susan.

~ 3 ~

"What do you think?"

Annie held up the beginnings of her Maine sweater for everyone to see. She had worked on it all weekend and had made good progress.

"That's really nice." Gwen stilled the clicking of her knitting needles to give Annie's creation her full attention. "Looks like it'll be warm too."

Alice fingered the worsted yarn and grinned at Annie. "That'll be warm enough for a Maine winter."

"Oh, good!" Peggy dropped the quilt block she was appliquéing and clasped her plump hands together. "Annie's decided to stay."

"Hold on! Hold on!" Annie laughed and shook her head. "You're all going to hurt yourselves jumping to conclusions like that."

Mary Beth nodded wisely. "You're making a sweater, not a commitment, right, Annie?"

"Exactly."

"Well, we'd like you to stay." Kate shyly lowered her head and went back to work on the delicate crocheted vest she had almost finished. "It's been so nice having you here."

Annie beamed at the younger woman and went back to work on an azure stripe in her sweater. "I've loved being here. I guess getting Grey Gables fixed up and decluttered has been more of a job than I expected, but getting to know everybody here has been a nice fringe benefit. It kind of reminds me of when I used to visit here in the summers when I was young."

With a hint of a smile, Alice made a French knot in the intricate floral bellpull she was cross-stitching. "When you and Susan Morris were such good friends."

"I'm sorry, Annie," Mary Beth said. "We never finished our chat about her."

"Susan Morris?" Gwen tilted her blond head to one side, thinking. "I remember her. Didn't she lose her parents in a car accident?"

"Yeah, she did." Mary Beth sat in one of the comfy chairs in the circle of crafters and started sorting out a large box of embroidery floss for her store display. "She'd just come back from college and was living at home again when her mother and father were killed. It must have been so terrible for the poor girl."

"I had no idea. Poor Susan." Annie had met Susan's parents only a couple of times, but she knew how close to them Susan had been. What had her life been like after their loss? "You don't know what she did next, do you?"

"I thought she went off and married some rich guy." Gwen pulled more yarn from the ball in her knitting bag. "Can't remember his name now; it's been so long."

"That's right." Mary Beth bit her lip. "What was his name? He was some bigwig in shoes or something like that. I could pick him out if I saw the name again. Anyway, she sold the family home, that house way out on the far end of Elm Street, and left to get married. Never came back to

Stony Point as far as I've ever heard."

"I knew her parents." As usual, Stella had been nearly silent for most of the meeting, but now she shook her regal gray head, not looking up from her knitting. "That house had been in the Morris family for almost 200 years, but young people, well, they don't understand what family means anymore."

That was just like Stella, and in spite of herself Annie smiled a little.

"I don't know. From what I remember, Susan loved that old house. She always said she never wanted to leave it. Ever. I guess Prince Charming, whoever he was, had other ideas about living in little Stony Point."

"I wonder if that's the house where the other handyman in town lives. He's way out on Elm, I know that much." Peggy stopped to cut out another piece of fabric to add to her appliqué flower. "Sometimes, when somebody needs a handyman and Wally already has a job, he has them call this guy. His name is Tom something. Maxwell, I think. Of course, until now, there hasn't been enough work to keep Wally busy."

"Until now?" Gwen asked.

"Wally got a job installing kitchens for a builder in Newcastle. Should be pretty steady work for a few months. Maybe more."

"Darn."

Everyone looked up at Mary Beth, and her face turned a little pink.

"Oh no, I don't mean I'm not happy for you and Wally, Peggy." She patted the younger woman's arm. "I was just hoping he could put in my new cabinets. That is, if the place I ordered them from ever gets me the right ones."

Annie shook her head. "Didn't you get that straightened out yet?"

"As far as I can tell. The guy promised they'd send a truck sometime this week to pick up the wrong ones and deliver the right ones. If they do, I'd like to get them installed as soon as possible."

"I hope so." Kate frowned. "All the new inventory and extra supplies are such a mess down there."

"And that's exactly why I want these new cabinets. A place for everything, and everything in its place."

"And when he's through with his other obligations, Wally can come work for me again." Annie finished up the azure stripe and fished in her bag for her crimson yarn. "He did a great job on my kitchen, and I'm going to have him work on the upstairs bathroom once I decide what I want done."

"Really?" Peggy's eyes lit up. "That would be great. Maybe we'll be able to put a little money aside for once. You know how tight finances have been for us lately."

Kate sighed. "Tell me about it. At least your Emily is still little. Vanessa will be wanting to go to college before long, and I don't know how I'm going to swing that on my own."

Everybody knew Kate's ex-husband Harry was unreliable. No wonder she didn't feel she could count on his help with their daughter.

Mary Beth gave her a motherly hug. "One day at a time, hon. That's about as much as any of us can really handle."

"Yeah, I know." Kate smiled. "One day at a time and a few good friends."

And they were good friends. Annie blinked hard, clearing the mist out of her eyes so she could see her crochet hook again. These were good people, and she was glad to know them all. Still, she couldn't help wondering who had been there for poor Susan after her parents' accident, and if she had friends who cared about her now. Well, wherever she was, she couldn't be that hard to find.

Annie started crocheting again, the rhythm of her hook brisk and determined.

* * * *

When the club meeting finally ended, Annie and Alice stopped for a quick lunch at The Cup & Saucer, and then Alice had to hurry off to her Princessa jewelry party. Annie went next door to the library.

Grace greeted her at the Circulation Desk. "You're back. How's that decorating book?"

"It's got some wonderful ideas in it. I'm going to do my bathroom over."

"Good idea. I love our old homes, but there's nothing like a sparkling new bathroom, even if you give it an old-fashioned look."

"Exactly. And I plan on spending more time looking through your section of books on decorating when I have the chance, but I really came in to ask you about city or state records. Marriages and deaths and that kind of thing. How would I look up something like that?"

Grace smiled. "That's quite a change from decorating. Are you researching your family history?"

"I'm still trying to find my friend Susan Morris."

"Any leads yet?"

"I've heard that she came back here after she went to college, that her parents were killed in a car accident, and that she sold their house and married a rich man who has something to do with the shoe business."

The laugh lines around Grace's blue eyes crinkled slightly. "I guess that's a start. How about we check the newspapers? If her parents were in an accident, there was probably an article about it somewhere. Do you know when it was?"

Annie considered for a minute. "Susan probably finished high school in 1984 and college in 1988 or so. I'd guess her parents died in '88 or '89."

"Unfortunately, the articles in *The Point* aren't indexed. Unless you want to go through a couple of years' worth of microfiched back issues, you might want to check the state's death records on the Internet first. When you have a date of death, you can see what the paper had to say about it. Come on back to the Reference Room with me. We'll see what we can find."

Annie followed her across the main part of the library into the room that housed the reference books, computers, and microfiche readers. It was a school day, so most of the computers were unoccupied. Annie sat down at one.

"Any suggestions on where to start?"

"Try the state of Maine death records," Grace advised. "And let me know if you get stuck."

"Thanks."

Grace gave her a little wave and disappeared back into

the library's Great Room. Annie stared for a moment at the computer screen. *The whole state of Maine, huh?* She took a deep breath and plunged in; "state of Maine death records" brought up the state's official website and a list of items for genealogical research, including "Index of Maine Deaths, 1960–1996." OK, maybe this wouldn't be one of those needle-in-a-haystack searches. In fact, it was kind of fun so far.

She clicked on the death index and was rewarded with a page that would let her input the name, town, and dates she was looking for. *All right, let's try this out.* She typed in "Morris" and "Jack" and "Stony Point," giving the date range as 01/01/1988 through 12/31/1989. *That ought to be close enough.*

Immediately one record popped up: *MORRIS, JACK L. - 8903367 - STONY POINT - 4/19/1989 - 48 years.*

Annie felt a sudden sadness. She had hardly known Mr. Morris, but he had died so young. About Wayne's age when he'd had his heart attack. Too young. Far too young.

She repeated the search process for Susan's mother with the same speedy result: *MORRIS, ELLEN P. - 8903368 - STONY POINT - 4/19/1989 - 45 years.*

Too sad. Too sad.

OK, plenty of time for getting all emotional later on. Business now.

She had used the microfiche reader before, so it didn't take her long to find the April 20, 1989, edition of *The Point*.

LOCAL COUPLE KILLED IN TRAFFIC COLLISION
by Robert T. Adkins
PORTLAND — Lifetime Stony Point resident, Jack

Morris, 48; and his wife, Ellen Morris, 45; were killed yesterday afternoon when their 1985 Chevy Blazer was struck by another vehicle. The driver of the other vehicle, whose name is being withheld pending notification of next of kin, also died at the scene of the accident. According to the Portland police, the ongoing investigation indicates that hazardous road conditions caused by yesterday's heavy thunderstorms may have been a contributing factor in the collision. The Morrises are survived by their daughter, Susan, also of Stony Point.

It was just a stark little article on the middle page of the paper where they put the fillers. With a sigh, Annie printed out a copy of the page and of the obituary that ran two days later. Apart from being listed as surviving the couple, there were no other mentions of Susan.

"How's it coming?" Grace asked when she came back into the Reference Room.

Annie showed her the printouts. "That's all I've found so far."

"Why don't you check the records on when she sold the house?"

"That's a great idea. Any suggestions on how I'd do that?"

"Look up the Lincoln County public records. There should be some information on their site."

Annie went back to the computer. From the several possibilities that appeared, she settled on the one that said "Lincoln County Registry of Deeds." When the site came up, she browsed around until she found a place where she could enter Susan's name and a date range from January

1989 through December 1990.

Several records popped up, but it was the third one from the bottom that made Annie smile. *MORRIS, SUSAN S. - BLANCHARD, PAUL & JUDITH - Deeds - Stony Point - 07/26/1989 - 1564-101.* So Susan had sold the house in July of that year. Now what about the marriage records? If she had married around the time she sold the house, it should be easy to find the name of her husband.

Annie wrote down the information from the deed registry, but just as she was about to start looking for marriage records, Grace's voice came over the intercom. "The library will be closing in five minutes. Please return all reference materials to the Reference Desk. If you have items you would like to check out, please bring them to the Circulation Desk now. Thank you, and please visit the Stony Point Library again soon."

Annie glanced at her watch. Five minutes till five o'clock already? The Internet could eat up time faster than anything she could think of. At least she had found out a few things, and she had some actual dates to go on. It was a start.

She picked up her purse and the microfiche copies she had made and went into the main part of the library. Several people were waiting to check out books, so she gave Grace just a wave and a smile before going out to her car. She had a feeling she'd be back soon enough.

When she pulled up in front of Grey Gables, she saw the red Mustang parked in the driveway next door and decided to drop in. Alice opened the door, stylish in a black sweater set that must have set off her line of jewelry to perfection.

"Annie!"

"Hey, neighbor. You busy?"

"Never too busy for you, neighbor." Alice smiled and opened the door wider so Annie could come in. "Just got back from my Princessa jewelry party, and I have one for Divine Décor in a little while, but I was taking a break for a few minutes."

"Oooh, it feels good in here." Annie rubbed her hands together, glad to be inside the carriage house's cozy living room.

"We may have a little more snow tonight. Have a seat. You want coffee? I have some on."

"That'd be great."

It took Alice only a minute to return with two steaming cups of coffee and a little plate of peanut butter cookies.

"I made these for the Princessa jewelry party. Might as well finish them off."

Annie took one. "How did it go?"

"Pretty well, actually. Sales are always up when Christmas is coming. How was the library? Find out anything?"

Annie handed Alice the newspaper report about the death of Susan's parents and their obituary. "Gwen was right about Mr. and Mrs. Morris, and Susan did sell the house in 1989."

"You're a regular Sherlock Holmes as usual. And the husband?"

"I didn't get a chance to look into the marriage records yet. But I'll see what I can find out at home. Grace was really helpful in showing me where to look, though. I may have to go back to the library. We'll see."

"Isn't there someone else in Susan's family you could contact? A niece or an uncle or a cousin or something?"

"I don't think so." Annie took a bite of the cookie she had taken. "Delicious as always."

"Thanks."

"Anyway, I don't think Susan had any family. I don't remember her talking about anybody but her mom and dad."

"Didn't she—?"

"Her aunt!" Annie clasped one hand to her forehead. "Of course, the one she stayed with when she lived in New York. It's so obvious, it never even occurred to me. Her return address has to be on some of those letters Susan sent me back in school."

"See? That haystack just got a lot more manageable. All you have to do is get back on the Internet and do a reverse lookup on that address, and more than likely it will tell you the name and telephone number of whoever lives there. Easy peasy."

"Easy for you, maybe. But thanks for the suggestion. I'll see what I can find out." Annie beamed at her. "I knew you were my best friend for a reason. I think Susan must have mentioned her aunt's first name in one of the letters, too, and I'm almost positive her last name was Morris."

"Just think, you might have Susan's phone number by tomorrow afternoon."

"That would be great. I don't know why, but I really would like to talk to her again and know that she's OK."

"Why wouldn't she be?"

Annie shrugged. "I don't know. I'd just feel better if I knew for sure. She always seemed to want so badly for somebody to be her friend. I don't like to think of her being alone in the world."

Alice reached over to squeeze her hand. "You were always nice to her. Not like me."

"You?" Annie shook her head. "OK, maybe the two of you were never best friends, but I don't remember you being mean to her or anything."

"Maybe not mean, not really, but I was always jealous."

"Really?"

"Oh, you know. The two of you spent so much time together, and your grandmother was always having her over. I guess I felt a little left out sometimes. And Susan was tall and graceful, just like I wasn't."

Annie smiled. "Neither of us has ever been what you could describe as tall, and both of us had our clumsy days."

"And I guess I was jealous of her looks too." Alice stared regretfully into the depths of her coffee cup and then took a drink. "All that blond hair."

"You could get a wig."

Alice laughed and half choked. "You would have to say that right when I took a big swallow."

"Sorry about that." Annie didn't quite suppress a giggle. "I was going to tell you not to feel bad, because we've grown up some since that time." She winked. "But maybe not."

"Just for that, I'm turning you out into the cold."

"Oh, I forgot." Annie drained her coffee cup and popped the rest of her cookie into her mouth. "Divine Décor, right? Where is it tonight?"

"Camden. It's not that far, but I've never been to that part of town, and I want to make sure I get there on time."

Annie gathered up her purse and the printouts she had brought with her. "You've been a tremendous help, neighbor."

"Anytime." Alice went with her to the door. "And I want to know what you find out about the aunt in New York, OK?"

"Sure. Have fun tonight."

Annie waved and scurried back to her own front porch and into the house. It *was* getting colder. She took a few minutes to start a fire in the hearth and then looked through the day's mail. Then she opened the drawer in the end table next to the couch and took out the stack of Susan's letters.

She had read them over several times since she first discovered them, remembering the friends and happenings Susan had written about, looking for clues they might hold. Was there any use in reading them over again? Something she had missed?

She ruffled the corner of the yellowing envelopes and saw the return addresses on each of them flip past. Many of the letters had been mailed from Susan's aunt's house in New York, but several were from 214 Elm Street in Stony Point.

What was the house like now? Annie remembered it being a huge white building, very old, very square and straight, with black-shuttered windows and a pretty little fan-shaped window above the front door. Like Grey Gables, it had two stories plus a large attic full of places to explore and to hide in. She hoped for Susan's sake that this Tom Maxwell had kept it nice. Being a handyman, he should.

Maybe she'd drive out and look at the old place again one of these days. It had been pretty old when she visited Susan there. No matter what kind of shape it was in now, it would be worth looking at.

In the meantime, Annie would keep working on her

Maine sweater. Winter was just around the corner now. Even during the day, she had to turn up the heat. The sweater would be a necessity before much longer, and she could use a nice peaceful evening by the fire to crochet and think. Tomorrow she'd do some more research and track down Susan once and for all.

4

"You're our first customer." Grace stood up from her station behind the Circulation Desk and walked with Annie over to the Reference Room. "Still looking for Susan Morris?"

"I'm working on it. I tried to do some searching on my laptop at home this morning, but I realized I don't have a clue what I'm doing." Annie took her notepad out of her purse and opened it up. "If you have a few minutes, I'd appreciate it if you could give me some pointers on looking up what I need."

"It can be a little overwhelming, can't it? There's so much to choose from."

"Exactly. If you could point me in the right direction, that would sure save me time."

"That's what I'm here for. Let's see what we can find."

Annie followed her into the reference area and sat down at one of the computers. Grace looked over Annie's shoulder at the screen.

"OK, what sort of information are you looking for today?"

"I'd like to know when Susan got married, and who her husband is."

Grace nodded. "The best place to start would be the state's marriage records. What else are you looking for?"

"She lived with an aunt in New York City when she went to high school. I'd like to find out where that aunt is."

"Did you try looking her up by name?"

Annie chuckled. "That's where the overwhelming part comes in. Do you know how many Kimberly Morrises there are in New York City? Alice told me you can get a phone number just by entering the address, but I don't know what kind of site that would be or how to find it."

"Supposing the aunt is still at the same address, you could try this white pages site and use their reverse lookup." Grace jotted the web address down on a piece of scratch paper and gave it to Annie. "It'll give you the phone number for the address you want and the name of the people living there. Provided it's not unlisted, of course."

"That's perfect. I really appreciate it."

Grace nodded. "And I'll be right up front if you need more help."

Annie thanked her and turned to the computer. She typed in "state of Maine marriage records."

The link took her back to the official state site and then to a marriage index. She entered the bride's name and town but left blank the fields for the groom's information. For the marriage date, she put in the entire year of 1989. "That ought to bring up Prince Charming." She hit Enter. A couple of seconds later, a message popped onto the screen: *No records found that meet your search criteria.*

Annie frowned. Maybe Susan hadn't gotten married as soon after she sold the house as everyone thought. Annie changed the date to cover 1989 through 1990 and hit Enter. *No records found that meet your search criteria.*

Maybe, since Susan had already sold the house, she hadn't listed her town as Stony Point. Annie cleared the box for the bride's town and hit Enter again. *No records found that meet your search criteria.*

Her frown deepened.

"Fine," she murmured and expanded the dates of the search to cover 1985 through 2005. "If Susan was married anywhere in Maine anytime within those twenty years, this will find her." *No records found that meet your search criteria.*

She went back to the browser and tried a few more sites, but those came up with nothing, wanted a written request for information, or charged for their services. Until she had a bit more to go on, Annie wasn't ready to go that route.

The marriage part was going to be a little more difficult than she expected. Maybe finding Aunt Kim would be a little easier.

She brought up the telephone directory Grace had suggested and entered the return address from Susan's New York letters. Almost instantly, she had a telephone number and a name. It wasn't Kimberly Morris as she had hoped, but it was a place to start.

"All right, Mayberry, Sheldon H., let's see what you know." Annie stepped outside to call the number on her cell phone and waited while it rang. And rang. And rang. Just as she was about to give up, there was a click on the other end of the line.

"Hello? Is that you, Carol Ann?" The voice clearly belonged to an elderly woman. "You were supposed to call me yesterday. You never called."

"I'm sorry, ma'am. This isn't Carol Ann." Annie felt a little bit guilty for the shortcoming. "My name is Annie Dawson. I'm calling—"

"No, I'm sorry, young lady, but you must have the wrong number. There's no Annie Dawson here."

"No, ma'am, my name is Annie Dawson. Are you Mrs. Mayberry?"

"Why, yes, I am." Annie could hear the smile in the old woman's voice. "Did Carol Ann ask you to call me?"

"No, I'm afraid I don't know Carol Ann. But I was wondering if you could answer a question for me."

"I'm not going to give you my Social Security number."

Annie had to force herself not to laugh at the sudden fierce determination she heard.

"No, ma'am. You shouldn't ever give that out to anyone. I'm just trying to find out about someone who used to live at your house a long time ago. I'm trying to find a friend of mine, and this lady was her aunt. Would you mind telling me how long you've lived there?"

"Let's see, it was November of 1988. I remember because it was Carol Ann's thirty-fifth birthday."

"You don't happen to remember who lived there before you, do you?"

Mrs. Mayberry laughed softly. "I let my husband take care of all the details. All I remember is we got the place because the lady who lived here had just passed away. Her name was Monroe or Morrison or something like that. I know it started with an M, because it was the same as our last name."

"Could it have been Morris?"

"Oh goodness, honey, it's been more than twenty years now. I couldn't say for sure."

"But you say the previous tenant had passed away back in '88?"

"That's what we were told. I'm sorry I can't be of any more help to you."

"No, Mrs. Mayberry, you've been a lot of help. I'm sorry to have disturbed you."

"You didn't disturb me at all, honey. You call back anytime."

Annie thanked her and hung up the phone. So much for finding Kimberly Morris there. Had she been the tenant who passed away in 1988? It was certainly possible.

After consulting with Grace once again, she spent a considerable amount of time trying to navigate the death records for the state of New York. Finally, she found a site used by genealogical researchers that claimed to have New York obituaries from 1988 forward. She typed "Kimberly Morris, 1988, New York City." That brought up forty-six different records, so she added "Jack" and "Ellen" to the search.

"Bingo."

There was a notice in the October 7, 1988, issue of the *New York Times*.

MORRIS — Kimberly Denise, 53. Staff Artist, Plus du Monde Chic. Died of complications of pneumonia at Columbia Presbyterian Medical Center on October 5, 1988. Survived by brother, Jack Morris; sister-in-law, Ellen Morris; and niece Susan Morris, all of Stony Point, Maine. She will be missed.

Poor Susan. Another loss. Annie knit her brows and tried to remember some of her high school French. *Plus du Monde Chic.* "More of the Fashionable World"? That sounded close enough. Aunt Kim must have worked for a small fashion magazine. What fun Susan must have had living with her while she went to high school.

Annie printed out a copy of the obituary. How terrible it must have been for Susan to lose her and then her parents so soon after.

"I wish you had let me know, Sooz. I'd have been there for you. I'd like to be there for you now."

"Fall down a rabbit hole?"

Annie started. "Grace. I didn't see you. My goodness, what time is it?"

"Almost two o'clock. I've been to lunch and back. You ought to take a break before you waste away back here."

"Maybe you're right. I still haven't found what I'm looking for, but thanks to you, I'm inching closer."

"Go get some lunch and a breath of fresh air. We'll still be here when you're ready to start looking again."

Air was exactly what Annie needed, the brisk October air out on Main Street. She stepped out of the library door, took a deep breath, and then scurried across Oak Lane to The Cup & Saucer. The lunch crowd was gone, and Annie was glad to see that her favorite corner table was empty.

Peggy looked up from the counter where she was refilling salt shakers. "Hi, Annie. What'll it be?"

"Coffee to start with. I don't know what I want to eat yet, but I'm starved."

It took just a minute for Peggy to bring her a steaming cup.

"Everything OK?"

"Yeah. It is." Annie sighed. "Some people just have it rough, you know."

"Sometimes you're the windshield; sometimes you're the bug."

Peggy gave her a menu and a wry grin, and Annie answered with one of her own.

"I know, but some people get a lot of trouble all at once."

"Anybody I know?"

"Susan Morris, the one we were talking about at the club meeting. I've been over at the library doing some research. Mary Beth was right about her parents being killed in a car wreck, and I found out that the aunt she was living with in New York died not very long before that."

"That's too bad." Peggy leaned against the other side of the booth. "And she was just out of college then? What a shame. What about that rich guy? Did you find out anything about him?"

"I haven't found any marriage records for Susan yet. So far, Prince Charming is still a complete mystery."

"Did somebody say Prince Charming?" A lanky guy in a policeman's uniform got up from his stool at the lunch counter and sauntered over to Annie's table. "Are you looking for me, ma'am?"

Peggy pursed her lips. "Oh, go sit down and drink your coffee, Roy, and let the adults talk."

"Now, that's no way to treat your elders, Peg. Why don't you introduce me to your friend here? Not that everybody in Stony Point hasn't heard of pretty Annie Dawson."

Annie didn't know whether to be flattered or annoyed. She settled for skeptical. "Have they?"

"Yes, indeed."

Peggy snorted. "This is Roy Hamilton. Obviously one of Stony Point's finest."

"I haven't seen you around town," Annie admitted, shaking the hand he offered. "Are you new here?"

"Just hired on by Chief Edwards when Callahan retired. I was working in Newcastle until a little while ago, but I heard Stony Point was a pretty attractive place to hire on." He grinned at Annie. "Very attractive, if you ask me."

Annie refrained from rolling her eyes. "Do you live here in town?"

"I'm renting a beach house on Ocean, just north of Elm." His grin widened. "I guess that makes us neighbors."

"You must be at Mr. Cruz's. The little house with white trim and a porch swing?"

"That's the one. And, of course, everybody knows about Grey Gables. That's a big place for one little lady by herself."

"I don't live alone." Annie pretended not to notice the smirk on Peggy's face.

"You don't?" Roy's sandy eyebrows met in the middle of his forehead. "I heard you were a widow."

Annie smiled sweetly. "I am."

"And all your family lives back in Texas, right?"

"They do."

Roy chuckled. "You've got a dog."

"A cat," Annie admitted. "But she's the jealous type."

"Hmm. Maybe I'll have to try to win her over with some fresh salmon. We lawmen aren't allowed to accept bribes, but that doesn't mean we can't offer a few."

She couldn't help laughing. "I'll leave that between you and Boots."

"Of course, if you'd like to …" A beep from the cell phone hooked to his belt drew his attention. "Excuse me a second."

He walked back over to the counter to take his call, and Peggy shook her head.

"Sorry about that, Annie. He's not one to take a hint."

"Poor guy's probably just lonely. It's hard when you're new in town. I know."

"I beg your pardon, ladies." Roy came back to Annie's table. "I've got business to see to, Annie, but I hope, now that we've been properly introduced, that I'll see you again."

"Stony Point's a small place." Annie kept her voice light and impersonal. "So that's pretty likely."

"Us being neighbors and all." Roy took his mirrored sunglasses from his shirt pocket. "If you ever need anything, you come see me. Thanks for the coffee, Peg."

He handed Peggy a folded bill and went out the front door. Annie watched as he took long strides across Main Street toward the town hall.

"Well, he's not shy."

"Just a nuisance more than anything else." Peggy made a sour face. "He's always asking for his 'police discount.' Hardy-har-har." Peggy unfolded the bill, brightening when she saw it was a five. "But he does tip well."

Annie chuckled, and Peggy pocketed the money.

"Anyway, back to what we were talking about earlier: I've been asking just about everybody I've seen if they know anything about Susan Morris, but nobody seems to remember much about her. Sorry. I really would have thought you'd find something about her marriage."

Annie sighed. "That's where I hit a brick wall. Nothing on any Susan Morris getting married to anyone anywhere in the state of Maine anytime between 1985 and 2005. Absolutely nothing."

"Hmm. I guess it's possible she was married somewhere out of state."

"I guess so." Annie took a sip of coffee. "That proverbial haystack just got a lot bigger. Are you sure you never heard anything about this man she was supposed to be married to?"

"Me? I was way too young to pay any attention to that kind of thing back then. Maybe Mary Beth will have thought of his name by the time you see her next."

"Or that shoe company he had. It was shoes, right?"

"That's what she said."

Annie bit her lip. "I guess I could search for Maine shoe manufacturers and see what I come up with."

"But if she wasn't married in the state, maybe he didn't live here either. His company could have been in Virginia or New York or Timbuktu."

Annie propped her chin on her hand. "Yeah, I know."

"Hey, I forgot." Peggy tapped the tabletop with one bright pink fingernail. "I have some good news for you. I asked Wally about the other guy, the handyman. His name is Tom Maxwell, and Wally says he'd do you a good job if you're in a hurry to start on your bathroom."

"Actually, I'd really rather have Wally do it. I know the kind of work he does, and that way it helps you out too.

But Mary Beth sounds like she doesn't want to wait much longer to get her basement organized. I'm sure she'd like the referral."

"I appreciate your wanting to hire Wally. I would like to see us get a little ahead for once."

"It's pure selfishness on my part. He did such a nice job on my kitchen, I don't want to use anyone else." Smiling, Annie handed the menu back to Peggy. "I hope you still have that shrimp chowder you had as your special today. I need something to warm me up."

"Coming right up."

~5~

The chowder was delicious, a hearty cream base packed with shrimp, bacon, and potatoes, and things looked a little bit brighter by the time Annie pulled up in front of Grey Gables.

Alice waved from the front porch of the carriage house and then scurried over to the car. "Find out anything?"

"You're just as bad as Peggy. Come in out of the cold, and I'll tell you about it." Annie unlocked her front door and picked up the stack of mail lying just inside. "I have some chicken and veggies in the slow cooker if you want to eat later on."

"That sounds a lot better than the leftover pasta I was going to have. Don't mind if I do."

There was a patter of paws on the stairs, and then Boots hurried into the room, rubbing against Annie's legs, demanding attention.

"All right. All right. You first." Annie handed Alice the obituary about Susan's aunt. "That's all I found out. Pretty much the end of the story as far as tracking Susan through her. Be right back."

When she returned from feeding the cat, Alice returned the article to her.

"End of story all right. I'm sorry."

"Now I just have to figure out how to track Susan down

through her marriage in 49 other states."

"Don't forget the territories, the District of Columbia, and all the foreign countries in the world."

"Great. Thanks." Annie sat on the couch beside Alice and started shuffling through the mail. "Bills, bills, and bills, it looks like. What did you decide about the harvest banquet?"

"It's the pumpkin bread again." Alice sighed dramatically. "My public demands it."

"You know you could always …" Annie frowned at the envelope she held. "I wonder what this is. It couldn't have come in the mail. There isn't an address."

Alice shrugged. "Maybe somebody brought it by. What's in it?"

"Let's see."

Annie slit open the envelope and took out the single sheet of paper, half smiling as she looked at it. The letters were cut from the newspaper the way they did in old gangster movies. It had to be a joke, right?

Alice's eyes showed her concern. "What is it?"

Annie let her read the message for herself.

FORGET ABOUT SUSAN AND MIND YOUR OWN BUSINESS.

* * * *

"Mayor Butler's office. May I help you?" Silver-haired Mrs. Nash waved at Annie and then spoke into the telephone receiver attached to her ear. "Yes, Mr. Price. Can you hold, please?"

She touched a button on the telephone on the desk and then smiled.

"Good morning, Mrs. Dawson. What can I do for you?"

"I was hoping to see the mayor." Annie cringed inwardly. This whole thing seemed so silly now. "I—I don't know whether it's important, but I'd sure like to talk to him about something."

"Hold on a minute." Mrs. Nash touched another button on the telephone. "Mr. Butler, Mr. Price is on line 1, and Mrs. Dawson is here to see you." She paused a moment. "Yes, sir, I'll tell her."

"I can come back if this is a bad time," Annie offered. "It looks like he's pretty busy."

"He wants you to go right in." Mrs. Nash gestured toward the door to the mayor's office and then returned to the call she had placed on hold. "Mr. Price? The mayor would like to know if he can return your call in a few minutes."

Ian opened the door before Annie could reach it, enveloping her hand in both of his.

"Come in, come in. Have a seat." He closed the door after her and then rolled a padded leather chair up to the desk and offered it to her, his dark eyes warm. "Nothing like starting the morning with a visit from a pretty lady."

She sat down, managing a little bit of a smile. "I'm really sorry to bother you with something so silly, but I just wasn't sure if this was something the police should see."

She handed him the anonymous note and waited for him to look it over.

He narrowed his eyes. "When did you get this?"

"It must have been pushed through my mail slot

sometime yesterday. I don't know when. I was in town most of the day."

"Looking for information on this Susan, right?"

"You've been at The Cup & Saucer."

"Word does get around." Ian put the note down on his desk. "Who touched this after you opened it?"

"Just Alice. And you, of course. That's all. I suppose I should have put it in a plastic bag or something to protect any fingerprints that were on it. It … well, it's kind of hokey looking, don't you think? I'm not sure if it isn't somebody's idea of a joke. As you said, word does get around. I have to admit, though, it creeped me out a bit to be all alone in the middle of the night."

"That's understandable. Where was it in the mail you picked up? On the top or the bottom?"

Annie shrugged. "I don't remember. I was shuffling through all the letters and telling Alice about the stuff I got on Susan from the library and didn't pay attention. Does it matter?"

"Maybe not. I just thought that it might give us an idea about whether it came before or after the regular mail delivery. What exactly did you find out about this woman, anyway?"

"Not much, really. Her parents and her aunt are the only relatives I know of, and they all died back in the late '80s. I'm still trying to find out who Susan married back then, but so far that's it."

"Nothing strange about the deaths?"

"Not at all. Her parents were in a car accident, and her aunt died of pneumonia. It's tragic, especially for a young girl suddenly left alone, but not mysterious. Now, though, I'm wondering why someone would take the trouble to leave me that message, and whether there's more to the story."

Ian looked at her for a long moment. "I don't like it."

"Do you think there's really anything to worry about? The note doesn't include any actual threat."

"No, I suppose not, but it just doesn't seem like something one of our people would do as a joke." He reached across the desk for her hand. "I want you to let me talk to the police chief about this."

She hoped he didn't feel the little shiver that ran through her. "You—you don't think it's that serious, do you?"

Laughing, he patted her hand and then released it. "Not serious enough for you to get worried about, OK? I just want to see what he says. Doesn't have to be anything official. If it's somebody we know who suddenly thinks he's a comedian or something, we can quietly put a stop to it. How's that?"

"Yeah, I suppose that would be the best way to handle it. Do you know someone who could look into it without making it a federal case?"

"Do I know someone? I'm a politician, remember?"

Annie beamed at him. "You're a good friend too. Thank you."

"Chief Edwards is just down the hall. I'll ask him about it and let you know." He raised one eyebrow. "You and Alice might have to have your fingerprints taken."

"That really *would* give folks something to talk about."

She stood up, and he followed suit.

"I'll let you know what I find out. You, um ... I was

thinking of going over to the Fish House for lunch in a little while. You want to come?"

That guileless charm was hard to resist, especially when combined with those rugged good looks. No wonder the voters loved him.

She squeezed his hand. "Give me a rain check, will you? I have a million things to do today. I have to go over to Malone's to pick out some paint colors first of all."

"More remodeling?"

"I want Wally Carson to work on my upstairs bathroom when he gets a chance. Though I guess I could get that other guy, Tom Maxwell, but I don't know anything about him."

"I've met Tom a time or two. Seems all right to me. He and his wife Sandy keep to themselves pretty much though, and I think most of the work he gets is outside town. Come to think of it, the Maxwells live in the old Morris house. Just for the past few years, though, so I'm afraid they couldn't help you out about Susan."

"I may just go out there and have a look around, anyway. For old times' sake."

"If you have to, but keep your eyes open when you're out and about. If you think anybody's acting strange around you, let me know or go straight to the police. OK?"

Annie glanced at the unevenly pasted letters on the note that lay open on Ian's desk. It was just a piece of paper. She wasn't going to let it become more than that.

"I'll be fine, Ian. Thanks."

*   *   *   *

The old Morris house was mostly the way Annie remembered it, even down to the fan-shaped window above the front door, but it was much smaller than she recalled from her girlhood. Still, it was a lovely old place set back in the trees, crisp and white against the brilliant reds and yellows of the maples. Susan had told her once that the house was nearly 200 years old. It had seen a lot of living. No wonder Susan had loved it.

Annie stopped at the end of the long gravel driveway and got out of the car, content to just look. She noticed that the door, like the shutters, was painted a very dark green, not the black she remembered from Susan's days, but the paint was fresh and neat, and the yard, apart from the wilder part that stretched back into the forest, was well kept. Maybe the Maxwells loved the house too.

She walked a little farther down the drive, lost in the memories of girlhood, remembering where she and Susan had played and giggled and whispered. She wandered up to the big oak at the corner of the house that had once held a tire swing. The swing itself was gone now, but the hooks that had supported the chains were still buried in place. And there were still some weathered strips of wood fastened to the tree trunk with long-rusted nails. She was sure they were the remains of the ladder Susan's dad had made to help them get up into the lower branches of the tree.

She and Susan had always pretended they were far above the earth, playing in the clouds like ...

"Did you want something?"

Annie sucked in a startled breath and turned. The man standing there in jeans and a rumpled flannel shirt open over a V-neck undershirt was perhaps in his late forties. His tangled mop of dark hair and serious stubble of beard told Annie that he had just wakened.

"I—I'm sorry. I was just—" She smiled weakly. "There used to be a swing in this tree."

He glanced up at the empty branches and then looked back at her, his eyes skeptical, suspicious. "Was there something you wanted?"

"Are you Tom Maxwell?"

"Yeah. Is that a problem?"

She blinked at his bluntness. "I'm so sorry. I didn't mean to disturb you."

He raked one hand through his hair. "It's no big deal. Did you want something?"

She tried the smile again. "My name is Annie Dawson. It sounds a little bit silly now that I'm here, but a friend of mine and her family used to live in this house about twenty years ago. I've been trying to find some information about her for a while now. Susan Morris."

"I don't know anything about twenty years ago. I bought the place from some people called Blanchard in 2000."

"Yes, I realize that, but—"

His dark eyes narrowed. "How would you know who I bought my house from?"

"Well, I didn't really know who you got it from, but I did find out that my friend sold it to the Blanchards back in 1989, so I just assumed …"

Annie let the words trail off. Clearly Mr. Maxwell was not impressed by her sleuthing abilities. She tried again.

"Don't you do handyman work in the area?"

"Yeah. Do you have something you need done?"

"I might. I'm thinking of redoing my bathroom, but I just can't decide exactly how. This is a great old house. Have you done any remodeling since you've been here?"

His suspicious expression did not change. "Some."

"I hope you didn't do very much. It's such a lovely old place."

"Not much."

"I guess Mrs. Maxwell likes having her own live-in handyman."

He shrugged. "When she doesn't have to wait for one of my other jobs to get done. How do you know about my wife?"

"I was just talking with Ian Butler. He said he'd met you before, and that you and your wife live out here."

His eyes narrowed again. "Why?"

"It was just small talk. We were discussing my friend and this house. It wasn't really about you and Mrs. Maxwell."

"I didn't think the mayor knew that much about us."

"Oh, Ian knows everybody in and around town. You'd like him if you got to know him. I think you'd like most everybody in Stony Point. Reverend Wallace always says— Have you met Reverend Wallace?"

"A time or two. Nice guy."

"Anyway, he always says that our neighbors are like—"

"Look, Mrs. Dawson, we pretty much think that a good neighbor is one who stays out of everybody else's way. Your friend sold this house years before I ever moved here, and I don't know all that much about the place anyway. It's a good solid house, and that's all that matters to me. I just can't help you with anything else."

He crossed his arms over his chest and looked pointedly in the direction of her car.

"Do you think your wife—?"

"I think my wife can't help you either. We're both pretty busy. I'm sure you can understand that."

Obviously, the conversation was over. Shoulders sagging, Annie thanked the man and got back into her car. She backed up a little bit so she could turn around in the drive. As she did so, she took one more look at the house.

A woman peered out of the window and then disappeared, perhaps when she realized Annie had seen her. Despite Mr. Maxwell's flinty expression, Annie waited a moment more, but didn't see anyone else. Finally, she pulled away from the house and headed for home.

Obviously the woman was Mrs. Maxwell, but why hadn't she come outside?

And why didn't she ever come into town?

~6~

"Hey, it's Alice. Call me when you get home. I want to ask your opinion about something."

Annie deleted the message and immediately returned Alice's call.

"What's up?"

"Hi. I just got my new Divine Décor catalog, and it has some darling little cornucopia centerpieces that might work great for the harvest banquet. Want to come look?"

"I might in a little while. I have to call LeeAnn back. She wants some ideas about what to get her husband for his birthday. And of course, Boots is demanding her dinner."

The cat was already rubbing against Annie's ankles, making assorted purrs and meows to entice her to come into the kitchen.

Alice laughed. "Naturally, the queen must be appeased. You sound tired. Everything OK?"

"Oh, I don't know. I went out to Susan's old house, out on Elm, and met Tom Maxwell."

"Really? Did you find out anything?"

"Only that he doesn't much care for nosy strangers poking around asking questions."

"No. He didn't actually *say* that, did he?"

"Not in words. But it was the weirdest thing. I'm sure his wife was looking out the window at me, but as soon as

I saw her, she disappeared. I wonder why."

"Maybe she wasn't dressed for company or something."

Annie considered that. "I suppose that might be the case. He was all rumpled and everything, as if he'd been asleep. Maybe she had been too. Still, I wish I could have talked to her. Don't you think it's weird that nobody in town really knows her? Does anybody ever even see her around?"

There was a shrug in Alice's voice. "I know I never have. But he doesn't seem to know anybody outside of his handyman work, either."

"Ian says he's met Tom before, and Tom said he knew Reverend Wallace, but what about his wife?"

"Did you ask him about Susan?"

"No, but I didn't expect him to know anything about her. She was gone long before he bought the house. But now I'm wondering what's going on with Mrs. Maxwell."

"Isn't one mystery enough for you? Or have you given up on the Susan thing?"

"Not hardly. I still want to find her." Annie nudged Boots out of the way and sat on the couch. "And I'd still like to know who put that note through my mail slot."

"What did Ian say about it?"

"He's going to ask Chief Edwards about it unofficially. It's probably not a big deal."

"Well, I'd say you had enough on your hands without stirring up things out at Tom Maxwell's."

"Still, I'd sure like to talk to Mrs. Maxwell myself. There's something strange about those two."

"You don't think he's one of those guys who doesn't want

his wife having any friends, do you, Annie?"

"I don't know. I'd go back out there and find out if I was sure he wasn't going to be home."

"I suppose if you knew somebody he was doing a job for, they could tell you when he was going to be working. But I don't know who."

"Alice, you're a genius! Peggy's already given his phone number to Mary Beth. She can arrange for him to install her cabinets, and while he's there, I can go make sure his wife is OK."

"Whoa, whoa, whoa. That's a pretty big conclusion to jump to just because a woman doesn't feel like meeting a total stranger who showed up on her property uninvited. And if there is something going on, don't you think you should let the police handle it?"

"They already think I'm crazy. Besides, I don't think he's holding her hostage or something like that. I just want to talk to her without worrying about him being around. It's not that scary."

"But, Annie—"

"I'm going to try to catch Mary Beth before the shop closes. Call you back in a minute."

She clicked off the phone and clicked it back on again. When she heard the dial tone, she punched in Mary Beth's number.

"A Stitch in Time. This is Mary Beth. How can I help you?"

"Hey there. It's Annie Dawson. I'm glad I caught you."

"Hello, Annie. What can I do for you?"

"Did you ever get your cabinets in?"

"As a matter of fact, they came today. The right model, the right color, and the right amount. It's a miracle."

Annie smiled to hear the relief in Mary Beth's voice.

"That's great. Do you have somebody to put them in for you yet?"

"I suppose I'll try that Tom Maxwell Peggy was telling me about since Wally's going to be busy for a while. Why? Do you know of somebody else?"

"No, actually I was hoping you were going to hire Tom. Um, it's kind of a weird situation …"

Mary Beth laughed. "It's not more about Susan Morris, is it?"

"No. Well, not entirely. Remember Peggy said she thought the Maxwells were living in Susan's old house?"

"Yeah. And?"

"I found out that she was right. I went out there, just for old times' sake more than anything else, and met Mr. Maxwell."

"What's he like?"

"He wasn't too happy to see me, I'm afraid. I don't think it was anything personal, but I think he had been napping when I showed up, and he was pretty grouchy."

Again Mary Beth laughed. "I don't blame him."

"Anyway, he wasn't going to introduce me to his wife, and he was pretty reluctant to say much of anything except that neither of them socializes much. I thought it sounded a little strange, and then, when I was driving off, I'm sure I saw her looking out the window."

"What's wrong with that?"

"Nothing, I guess. Maybe I'm looking for a mystery

where there isn't one, but I would really like to talk to her when he's not around. I thought maybe you could hire him to do your cabinets, and while he was over there, I could go introduce myself to her. Even if she doesn't feel like making a new friend, at least I could talk to her and make her feel welcomed."

"And you want me to hire this monster to work in my shop?" Mary Beth teased.

"I think he's probably all right. I mean, he's worked in the area for a long time according to Wally. I don't think Wally would recommend the guy if he was trouble, do you?"

"No, I think it's OK. Besides, it's just some cabinets, not a whole new kitchen or something, right? I'll give him a call to see when he can come out, and I'll let you know. And I hope there's nothing going on with Mrs. Maxwell that shouldn't be."

"Me too. Thanks, Mary Beth."

Boots was considerate enough to wait until Annie had hung up before she began demanding dinner again. This time Annie was sure she couldn't put her off.

"All right, come on. Anything to quiet you down, pest."

Annie scooped her up, snuggling her close until they got to the kitchen. Then, with Boots occupied with "a hearty seafood blend," Annie went back to the telephone and called Alice.

"We're set."

"You don't mean Mary Beth is in on this, do you?"

"Sure. Why not? She's going to call him up and see when he can come do her cabinets, and then she'll let me know. It's a perfect plan."

Alice made a little huffing sound. "You know, as much as there's probably nothing out of the ordinary going on over there, this whole thing is making me nervous."

"Don't make it into a big deal. I'll just go over and have a friendly chat with Mrs. Maxwell. If she's all right, that'll be the end of it. Maybe she'll even want to be friends. And if she does need help, I'd hate to think we all stood by and did nothing, wouldn't you?"

"Yeah, I suppose you're right. Once Mary Beth tells you when Tom's going to be at her place, let me know, and we'll go over to see his wife."

"We?"

"Yes, we." There was unshakable determination in Alice's voice. "You didn't think I was going to let you go over there by yourself, did you?"

"I don't think we both need to—"

"No arguments now. Either I go with you, or I call up Tom Maxwell and tell him everything."

"You wouldn't." Annie bit her lip. "Would you?"

"Absolutely. If your snooping gets you into trouble, it will be up to me to get you out of it. Or at least be right there in the middle of it with you."

"All right, you can come. But we're not going to make it a big deal. I just want to have a friendly chat with Mrs. Maxwell. Some people need a little extra encouragement, as Gram used to say. Then I will have done what I'm supposed to. Fair enough?"

"Fair enough. You let me know what Mary Beth says."

"All right. Have a good night."

Annie hung up the phone and was about to go fix herself

a sandwich when the phone rang.

"Hey, Annie. This is Ian Butler."

"Hi, there. What's going on?"

"Just wanted to let you know that I talked to Chief Edwards about that note you got. He had Officer Hamilton take a look. Evidently there are two different sets of distinct prints on it and some partials of a third. You and Alice both need to go see him so they can rule you out."

"All right."

"Of course, there's a good chance that those two sets of prints belong to you ladies, but we'll see. Maybe we'll get lucky anyway."

"Do I need to make an appointment with him?"

"No, he said just come by whenever you're in town. They'll take your prints, and then take it from there."

"OK." Annie hesitated for a second, thinking she'd tell him about her visit with Tom Maxwell, but she decided not to risk another lecture. "Thanks for talking to Chief Edwards for me, Ian."

"Anytime, Annie. I want to make sure you're safe."

Annie smiled as she hung up the phone. It was nice to have someone looking out for her.

*   *   *   *

Alice was busy all the next day, but Annie coaxed her into coming into town with her the day after that, promising to help her look for a new outfit at Dress to Impress, and then to treat her to a cup of coffee after they had gone to see the chief of police.

"I want something to go with that new line of faux opals and diamonds I just got in," Alice said as they pulled up to the town hall in her little red Mustang. "Something pastel, I think."

"That'd be pretty. Maybe a lavender or a baby blue." Annie smoothed her hair in the passenger-side mirror and got out of the car. "Thanks for doing this, by the way. I hope it won't take too much time."

"Not a problem. If there's a weirdo in town, I want to know who it is. Besides, it's kind of exciting having your fingerprints taken and being part of an investigation."

Reed Edwards looked more like a lumberjack than a police chief. The thought had crossed Annie's mind the first time she had met him, while he was coaching the softball team at the church picnic last summer. Now, when he stood up from behind his desk, towering over her as he swallowed up her hand in both of his, she couldn't help thinking it again. He was definitely the rugged, outdoor type, with a deep tan and sun-bleached hair to show for it.

"It's good to see you again, Mrs. Dawson."

He released her hand and took Alice's.

"Thanks for coming in, Alice, though I didn't expect to have either of you in here unless it was to get a permit to raffle off something at the church or get donations for the food pantry."

"I'm sorry it's not for something a little more pleasant than it is," Annie said.

Chief Edwards nodded. "Ian gave me the note and told me how you got it. Is there anything else I ought to know?"

"I wish there was something else I could tell you. Do

you think someone gave that to me as a serious warning?"

"It's hard to say, I'm afraid. You've been asking around town about this Susan Morris lately ..."

"You don't happen to know anything about her or her family, do you?"

"Sorry. That was well before my time. I did check our records, but there's nothing on any of the Morrises. As far as I can tell, they were all upstanding citizens."

Annie frowned. "Although that's good to know, it certainly isn't helpful at this point."

"Anyway, with you making your search public knowledge, it could be that our mystery correspondent knows something he'd rather you didn't dig up. Or, as Ian said, it could be somebody's idea of a joke. Either way, we'll see whether or not this person was careless." The police chief pressed a button on his telephone, setting off a buzzer in the room next door. "Hamilton?"

"Yes, Chief?"

"We're ready."

Roy Hamilton came in with all of his fingerprinting paraphernalia and grinned at Annie.

"So you came to see me after all."

Annie pursed her lips. "I couldn't resist."

Chief Edwards looked from Roy to Annie and back again. "I see you two have met."

"Briefly but memorably." Roy winked at Annie and then nodded to Alice. "Hello there. Been keeping busy?"

"As always. Business is booming."

"That's great. Well, we'll try to get this all done quickly. Wouldn't want you to miss a sale."

"Thanks."

"What do we need to do?" Annie asked as Roy took her hand.

"Let me have your first finger, right hand."

She extended the requested digit, and he rolled it on his ink pad and then on a little card with her name typed on it. The card had designated spaces for all ten fingers, which Roy filled with practiced ease.

"There you go, ma'am. Sorry to have soiled those lovely hands."

"Thanks for helping us out," Annie replied. "I just hope this isn't a waste of everybody's time."

"Not a problem." Roy began the fingerprinting process again, this time for Alice, although he was still directing most of his comments to Annie. "Stony Point tends to be pretty quiet most days. This gives us a little practice on procedure and with much better company than usual."

Annie kept her smile sincere and impersonal. It was the best way to deal with a flirt.

Finally, Roy handed Alice a paper towel to wipe the excess ink off her fingers. "I guess that'll do it for now. Anything else, Chief?"

Edwards shook his head. "Just let me know if the prints on the note belong to somebody besides the mayor or one of these ladies."

"Will do." Roy gathered up his things and nodded particularly at Annie. "See you girls around."

"Anything else we need to do?" Annie asked once Roy had gone.

"Not really, but do be careful. Here's my card. If you

get any more notes, any kind of communication at all that seems out of place to you, let me know right away. If you see anybody who's where he shouldn't be or who just feels wrong to you, let me know that too. Big or small, we can check it out."

"I really appreciate it." Annie put the card in her purse. "You guys are my heroes."

The police chief ducked his head a little. "It's what we're here for, ma'am."

"Thanks, Reed," Alice said. "Tell your mother I said hello."

"I will, Alice. You take care now."

Alice hurried Annie out of the building.

"I told you so. I told you he likes you."

Annie stopped short and put one hand on her hip. "What are you talking about?"

"Don't pretend you don't know. Roy Hamilton likes you."

"Oh yeah? Well, even if he did, and I'm not saying he does, are you trying to palm him off on me?"

Alice laughed. "I'm not trying to do anything. He's the one who's obviously smitten, like every other guy in town."

"You're such a comedian." Annie started walking again. "Who, exactly, is 'every other guy in town'?"

"You don't need to look any farther than that guy back there." Alice gestured toward the town hall. "Don't deny it now."

"You're crazy. I've hardly spoken to the chief before today. Besides, I'm sure I heard he's married."

"You know very well who I'm talking about, and it's not Reed Edwards."

"If you mean Ian, I'd have to conclude that you have an overactive imagination."

"I'm not the only one who's noticed."

Annie rolled her eyes. "Then they have overactive imaginations too. Ian and I are just friends. Is there any reason a grown man and a grown woman can't just be friends?"

"None at all, except when they aren't."

"OK, OK. If ever Ian and I aren't, you'll be the first to know. Deal?"

Alice grinned. "Deal. Now let's go shopping."

"Umm—maybe that's not such a good idea just this minute."

Alice's face fell. "What do you mean? You said we could go look at clothes and then have coffee. I was planning on some pie, too, if Peggy's got coconut."

"I don't think they'd really want us putting our hands all over the merchandise in our present condition." Annie held up her hands, displaying ten black fingertips. "Do you?"

"Hmm, maybe we'd better take a trip to the hardware store and see if they have some of that industrial-strength hand soap."

~ 7 ~

Things were quiet for the next couple of days. Annie looked for more information about Susan on her laptop computer at home, but she didn't find any useful information. And she hadn't had a chance to go back to the library for help in the search. Mary Beth hadn't yet made any definite plans for Tom Maxwell to install her cabinets, so Annie had to hold off on visiting Sandy Maxwell. Besides, she needed to take care of mundane things like laundry and cleaning from time to time. Gram wouldn't have stood for a less-than-tidy house.

Annie's twin mysteries were not uppermost in her mind when she picked up the mail from her entryway floor. Not until she saw the unaddressed envelope at the bottom of the pile.

"Somebody was here, and I didn't even notice."

She opened the front door, but the street was deserted. There wasn't even a dog in sight, but still she felt as if someone was watching her.

"Don't get spooked by this. It's just a note."

She made sure to lock the front door before sitting down on the living room couch. For a minute, she just looked at the envelope. It was blank like the first one.

She started to open it and then stopped. Yes, she had touched the envelope, but she hadn't yet touched the note on the inside. If there were fingerprints on it, they would belong to the author and no one else, right?

She took her purse off the hall table and rummaged in it until she found Chief Edwards' business card. She had only glanced at it when he gave it to her in his office two days before, but now she found something comforting about the no-nonsense block letters and the official Stony Point Police seal.

She punched in the phone number printed on the card and was relieved when someone answered on the first ring. "Stony Point Police, Officer Hamilton."

"Roy? This is Annie Dawson."

"Well, well, just the lady I was about to call. I have some news for you about that anonymous note you got."

"And I have some news for you. I just got another one. Is Chief Edwards in?"

"Actually, he's assigned your case to me."

"What do you want me to do?"

"What does this one say?"

"I haven't opened it yet." Annie looked at the envelope, searching for any kind of identifying mark. "I thought it would be better if I turned it over to you without tampering with it."

"Very good. And when did it come?"

"Sometime today. Before the mail."

"All right, don't do anything. I'm on my way over."

She exhaled. "Thanks, Roy. I'll be looking for you."

A few minutes later, he was at her door.

"The cavalry has arrived."

"Come in, Roy." She stepped back to let him into the house. "The note's in the living room."

They both went in and sat on the couch. She started to pick up the note, but he stopped her.

"Let's be careful with this one." He took some flimsy-looking latex gloves from his pocket and put them on. "Now, let's see what we have."

He opened the envelope and took out a single sheet of paper. Like the first, this one had a message made up of letters cut from the newspaper.

LEAVE THE PAST IN THE PAST.

He studied it for a moment. "Not much to go on in this one, either."

"It's got to be about Susan again. What about her past does this person not want me to find?"

"What time did this come?"

"Before the mail is all I know. I've been cleaning house, and I swept the entry at about nine thirty, so I know it wasn't there then. The mail usually comes between eleven o'clock and noon, and it was before that."

"OK, between nine thirty and noon. That doesn't really pinpoint it for us." He narrowed his eyes, inspecting the letters and the paper itself. "Seems like the same kind of paper as the first one. The same kind of envelope too."

She shook her head. "No, this is one of those safety envelopes, the ones you're not supposed to be able to see through. The first one was just plain."

"You're right at that." He grinned at her. "Have you ever considered going into police work?"

She couldn't help smiling back. "I think I stay busy enough as it is."

"You've certainly got somebody stirred up. I'm just glad

I'm the one looking out for you about it."

"And I appreciate it, Roy. I suppose you'll have to check this one for fingerprints."

"As soon as I get back to the office. Oh, I told you I had news about the first note. Besides yours and Alice's and a couple of smudges that belong to the mayor, there weren't any prints. Whoever passed it along was pretty careful. I'd be surprised if this one was any different."

"Great. Now what do I do?"

He patted her hand. "First thing, you don't worry. Like I said, I'm going to look out for you. All you have to do is let me do my job. If you get any more of these, or if you see or hear anything that makes you uncomfortable, let me know. I'll be right over."

"I really appreciate it." She stood up. "Do you need anything else from me?"

He smiled hopefully. "A cup of coffee might be nice."

"I wish I could, Roy." She made her smile polite but firm. "I'm right in the middle of cleaning my kitchen, and things are really a mess. Will you excuse me?"

He stood up. "All right. Maybe some other time?"

"We'll see."

"Meanwhile, I'll see what I can find out about this note and let you know. You know, by the time this is all over, you and I'll probably be pretty good friends."

"We'll see." She opened the front door for him. "Thanks for coming out, Roy."

"See you soon, Annie."

Once he was gone, she went back to cleaning the kitchen, glad she had a legitimate excuse for hurrying him on his way.

One of these days she would have to have a frank conversation with him about what she did and didn't see in her near future. For now, she was glad to have him on her side.

*   *   *   *

The next day, with Grey Gables clean enough to impress even Gram, Annie decided to try once again to find something about the man Susan had married. Or something, anything, about Susan herself. Maybe she would just try a random search. Who knew what she might get?

She booted up her laptop computer and opened a search engine.

"Here goes nothing."

She typed in "Susan Morris" and hit Enter.

Results 1–10 of about 74,600 for "susan morris." (0.28 seconds)

There was that haystack again, but she wasn't ready to abandon Susan quite yet. She tried several different search phrases with similarly overwhelming results.

"How about 'Susan Morris' and 'Stony Point Maine'?"

She tapped the keys and got just one result. It was a blog post from May 2002, and the blogger was waxing poetical about the summer of her fifteenth year, and how she had decided to experience everything she could during her lifetime, no matter how long or short it might be. With her brows knit together, Annie scanned the page. What did this have to do with Susan?

She found her answer about three-quarters of the way down the page.

I remember it, because that was the same day they were searching for a girl who had drowned off Folly Beach. I didn't know her, but the newspaper said her name was Susan Morris, and she was from someplace called Stony Point, Maine. I remember her name because I thought then that someone ought to remember it. Remember her. And I thought it was strange that she had come so far just to drown.

Tears burned in Annie's eyes. Drowned? Not Susan. Not after everything else that had happened to her. It wasn't fair.

Annie blinked hard and read the post again. The blogger gave only a first name, Maggie. Maggie of Maggie's Musings. No city. No state. No contact information. How long ago had the drowning been? Where was Folly Beach anyway?

It took only a second to look up Folly Beach, South Carolina. It was not far from Charleston. What newspaper did they have there?

She typed in "Charleston SC newspaper," and got the site for *The Post and Courier* and clicked the "Contact Us" link. There she found a list of names and e-mail addresses for various departments and then, at the bottom, a link that said "Archives."

"Oh, please, please be searchable."

She clicked the link and found "Search the archives" and "Advanced search." Yes.

She typed in Susan's name, but there were only two results. One was an article about healthy eating and the other was a death notice for a woman aged 83. Not her Susan.

Entering "Stony Point" returned articles on the local woods, a golf course, and a historic home.

How could this Maggie have read about Susan in the newspaper if there wasn't an article? And if there was an article, why wasn't it in their archives? Wait. The searchable archives went back only as far as 1994. Susan had sold her house in 1989, and maybe she had drowned later that same year. Would the newspaper be willing to send her a copy of the article?

She clicked on the link that said "More information about finding stories from *The Post and Courier*" and quickly decided against that idea. They wanted a pretty penny for doing research for anyone not on staff, but she was glad to see that the county public library had microfilm of all issues of the paper from 1931 through 1993. And they had kindly furnished a link.

She clicked through to the library's index and once again typed in Susan's name. In the field for "Pub Year" she typed in 1989. The search brought up one article, and she clicked on the box marked "Details." *Coast Guard and Charleston Rescue abandon search for Susan Morris of Stony Point, Maine, believed drowned off Folly Beach 08/24/1989*. The article titled "Search Halted for Maine Woman Believed Drowned" was dated August 27, 1989.

Annie pressed her hands against the sides of her aching head and realized it was far past lunchtime. A sandwich and a strong cup of coffee would be the best thing to pull her back into the present. Susan was gone, and regret wouldn't bring her back.

Annie printed out the information available about the article, including the contact number for the library. She would give them a call once she'd had a chance to process everything she'd found out so far. Maybe they'd send her a copy of the article and not expect her eyeteeth in return.

She thought for a minute. Maybe it would be better to talk to Grace again. Sometimes libraries exchanged information with each other more quickly than they did with Citizen Jane.

She spruced herself up and drove to the library. The Circulation Desk was deserted, so she tapped the little bell that was labeled "Ring for Assistance." A few seconds later, Grace came out of one of the back rooms.

"Annie, good to see you. I've been wondering how you were doing. Did you ever find your friend?"

"Yeah." Annie blinked hard. "I did. And I guess I found out more than I wanted to know."

"Bad news?"

"She drowned back in 1989, and I never even heard about it."

"That's too bad. What happened?"

Annie showed the librarian the information she had found so far.

"I was going to give the library there a call to see what they have on that newspaper article. Then I was thinking maybe you could get the information sent up here, and I wouldn't have to go all the way to Charleston for it."

Grace took the printout. "Let me see what I can do. If they're not too busy, they may be able to fax or e-mail me a copy right away, library to library."

"I was hoping you'd say that. It won't be too much trouble, will it?"

Grace smiled. "I told you, I know people."

Annie wanted to hug her for being so helpful. "Thanks

so much Grace! Anything you could get from them would be wonderful."

"Are you going to be in town for a while?"

Annie nodded. "I have some errands to take care of. Do you think it will be that quick?"

"I don't know for sure, but I'll see what I can do before you get back."

Annie ran her errands and even stopped in to chat with Peggy at the diner, catching her up on this most recent development. When she returned to the library, though, Grace didn't have any results for her. But by the next afternoon, she called to ask Annie to come see her.

"Success." She gave Annie a couple of pieces of paper. "A few years ago, I worked with a woman who's at the library in Charleston now. She was nice enough to e-mail me a copy of the article you wanted, as well as an earlier one on the drowning."

Annie glanced at the pages. "I really appreciate it. What do I owe you for them?"

"Oh, don't worry about that. She sent them to me as a favor, and I'm just passing them on. Sorry it had to be bad news, though."

"At least I know for sure." Annie sighed. "I was really looking forward to getting back in touch with Susan. I guess that'll teach me not to take any of my friends for granted."

"You never know how long you have with anyone. I guess we both know that too well." There was a touch of wistfulness in Grace's expression, and Annie remembered that she, too, was a widow. "But at least you tried to find her. That was thoughtful of you."

Annie thanked her one last time; then she went over to one of the overstuffed chairs in the reading area and sat down. The first article was dated August 22, 1989.

CHARLESTON   RESCUE   SEEKING   WOMAN MISSING OFF FOLLY BEACH

FOLLY BEACH – Last night, a woman disappeared from the yacht she and her fiancé were sailing down the coast to Florida. It is believed that the 22-year-old may have fallen overboard during the brief storm that blew into the Charleston area last night around midnight. Her fiancé told police that he was sleeping below deck and did not realize she was missing until early this morning. Authorities have not released the couple's names, but report that they had sailed from the Portland, Maine, area. The victim's fiancé was not immediately available for comment.

The poor man, whoever he was. What a terrible blow it must have been to lose Susan just as they were starting their life together.

Annie looked at the other article. It was the one she had originally requested from August 27 of that year.

SEARCH HALTED FOR MAINE WOMAN BELIEVED DROWNED

FOLLY BEACH – After the Coast Guard and Charleston Rescue abandoned search operations today, police released the name of the woman believed drowned off Folly Beach on August 21. She has been identified as Susan Morris, 22, of Stony Point, Maine. According to her fiancé, Archer Prescott, owner of sporting-goods manufacturing concern JFP Athletics Inc., the couple had been sailing down the coast to his estate in Vero Beach, Fla., for their wedding.

"I knew there was a little storm coming up, but it wasn't due for a while. The sea was quiet, so I went to my cabin for a nap," Prescott said. "It was pretty late. Susan told me she would keep watch and let me know if she needed me for anything. She had done it several times before, so I didn't think anything would go wrong. I guess I was more tired than I thought, because I slept right through the night. I'd never done that before. When I woke up and didn't find her on deck or anywhere below, I radioed the Coast Guard, but she was gone. Just gone."

A general alert along the North and South Carolina coasts, and to ships in the area has brought no results. Coast Guard Captain Michael Raintree, in command of the search operation, could offer no hope that Morris might still be alive. "Anyone alone out on the ocean has very little chance of being found, and that chance becomes smaller and smaller with every hour that passes. She was reported to be a strong swimmer, but even if that's the case, no one could last this long in open water. We would have been notified by now if another vessel had picked her up, or if she had reached shore. It's a tragedy, of course, to lose a young woman like that. We hate to have to give up, but experience tells us that there's nothing more we can do."

Prescott, however, was unwilling to accept the decision made by Charleston Rescue, the Coast Guard and others involved in the search. "I'm not giving up," he said. "If Susan's out there, if she's alive, I'm going to find her. And if, God forbid,

she's dead, I want to know that too. I can't just abandon her.
I'll never forgive myself for leaving her on deck like that, and I
owe it to her to keep looking. She's everything to me."

The couple's wedding was scheduled for today.

Annie closed her eyes for a minute. That was it, then. Susan was gone, and no doubt this Archer Prescott had picked himself up and moved on with his life. He was probably married to someone else and had kids—maybe even grandkids; 1989 was a long time ago.

She thought for a minute that she would go back to the Reference Room to see what she could find out about this JFP Athletics he owned, but the whole idea of following up on the lead didn't appeal to her anymore. It was done. It was over. Time to go home, feed the cat, catch up with LeeAnn and the twins, and work on her new sweater.

She gathered up her things, and with another quick thank you to Grace at the Circulation Desk, she went out to her car. Before she could get in, Peggy waved to her from the window of The Cup & Saucer. Then she held up her index finger, a gesture Annie took to mean Peggy wanted her to stay where she was.

Annie put the papers she was carrying and her purse on the front seat and waited until Peggy scurried out of the café.

"I can't stand the suspense. Did you find out Prince Charming's name?"

"The article says his name was Archer Prescott. Did you ever hear of him?"

Peggy thought for a minute. "I don't think so. Was he from somewhere around here? Couldn't have been Stony

Point. People would have remembered."

"I don't know. All I know is that when he knew Susan, he was the owner of JFP Athletics. Could be shoes, like Mary Beth said. I didn't really check them out."

"Oh yeah. I remember them. Wally used to have some of their work boots. He loved those old things. He always said they were the best he'd ever had and wouldn't throw them away for anything. They finally wore out on him, so he bought some more about five or six years ago. But those were awful. Too expensive, and they fell apart on him way too quickly. He said JFP was never the same after they moved the company out to the West Coast."

"That's a shame. Maybe this Prescott guy sold the business after Susan died. You never know."

"Yeah, I suppose not. Well, I'd better get back to work. We get a little rush around four o'clock or so. Some of the older folks like to get in and out before the evening crowd."

"Don't work too hard, Peg." Annie got into the car. "And thanks for asking around for me."

"Sure thing. Are you going to try to call the guy up? Maybe he can tell you more."

Annie shook her head. "I don't think there's much else to know. I wish I hadn't lost touch with Susan over the years. Maybe she wouldn't have been on that boat, and things wouldn't have ended up like this. Who knows?"

With a little wave, Annie shut her car door and drove down Main Street. Maybe Susan would have been somewhere else if she and Annie had stayed friends. And maybe Annie's own life would have been different too. No Wayne. No LeeAnn. No twins.

Annie chuckled to herself as she turned onto Maple Street. She could almost hear Gram telling her not to borrow trouble. *Who are you, missy, to think you're in control of how people's lives play out? Let God run the world. He's had a lot of practice.*

Annie slowed as she turned onto Ocean Drive and was treated to a wide view of the sea, of the deep sapphire water capped with foam that leaped and danced against the rocks to the music of the surf.

Too much gloom for one afternoon, she decided as she breathed in the fresh salt air, especially one as glorious as this. A gull took wing, soaring and disappearing into the sun, and Annie smiled. It was time to let Susan go.

~ 8 ~

But Annie couldn't let Susan go. Yes, she was gone, but Annie knew the name of the man she had planned to marry. Surely this Archer Prescott would be able to tell her something about Susan's last days, and whether they were happy. Maybe then she could move on.

Late that evening, once she had made up her mind, she looked up the contact information for JFP Athletics Inc. in San Diego. Listed as president and CEO was one Archer L. Prescott. Annie jotted down the company's telephone number and address. She'd just call the man. What could it hurt?

"You're as determined as your grandmother," her grandpa had often said, and Annie smiled to herself. Maybe she did have a lot of Gram's determination. Pigheadedness, Grandpa would have called it, and there would have been a twinkle in his eyes. But Gram never let anything stand in her way. Neither would Annie.

California was three hours behind them in Maine, so Annie had to wait until after noon of the next day before she could call the number for JFP Athletics. Even then, she was afraid she might be calling too early.

"Good morning, JFP. How may I direct your call?"

The voice on the other end of the line sounded very young. Annie couldn't help picturing her. Did they even call them "valley girls" anymore?

Annie put a smile into her voice. "Good morning. I would like to speak to someone in Archer Prescott's office."

"One moment, please."

Annie sighed, hearing the "easy listening" music that was supposed to entertain her while she held. Fortunately, the wait wasn't long.

"Mr. Prescott's office."

This voice was cool and professional, definitely older than the first. Absolutely.

There was nothing to do but plunge ahead.

"Good morning. My name is Annie Dawson. I'd like to speak to Mr. Prescott, if that's possible."

"May I ask to what this is in reference?"

"It's, um, it's a personal matter. May I speak to him?"

"I'm sorry, Ms.—?"

"Dawson. Annie Dawson."

"Ms. Dawson. I'm sorry, but I'm sure you appreciate how busy a man like Mr. Prescott is. Unless you can give me a little more information on the purpose of your call, I'll have to ask you to speak to someone in our Public Relations Department. They can deal with any requests for donations to charitable or political causes."

Annie shook her head even though the gesture couldn't be seen by the woman on the other end of the line. "I'm not trying to get a donation for anything. I'm trying to get some information about a woman Mr. Prescott was once engaged to—Susan Morris."

"I see." The woman's voice was coolly polite. "Has she asked you to contact him?"

"I'm afraid she passed away back in 1989, but I would like to talk to him about her."

"Mr. Prescott is in conference at the moment. May I ask him to return your call?"

"All right."

Annie managed to keep the disappointment out of her voice. After all, the owner of a big company didn't just sit around his office all day waiting to take calls from total strangers. She gave the woman her telephone number and repeated her name for good measure.

"If you'll just let him know I'm calling about Susan Morris, I would very much appreciate it."

"I will make sure he gets the message. Have a good day."

There was an abrupt click, and the call was over.

"I guess that's that."

Boots had been snoozing on the couch beside her, and now she yawned and stretched, nuzzling Annie's hand. Annie scratched behind the cat's ears and under her chin.

"What do you think, Miss Boots? Do you think he'll call me back?"

The cat only purred and blinked her eyes.

"We'd better have something for lunch, and then I have got to make some decisions about that upstairs bathroom."

By nine o'clock, when it was six on the West Coast, Annie gave up hope of having a call that day from Archer Prescott of JFP Athletics Inc. By the same time the next evening, she gave up hope of ever hearing from him at all.

*   *   *   *

The next day, Annie decided to stop by the mayor's office. Ian knew everybody in town. Maybe he knew something about Archer Prescott too.

"I wanted to ask your opinion about something," she said, once he had invited her to sit down.

"I heard you found out your friend had passed away."

"How did you—?" Annie shook her head. "Peggy again, right?"

Ian shrugged. "She likes to chat with the customers, you know."

"That won't make my mystery correspondent very happy."

"Chief Edwards told me they didn't find any evidence to track the guy down yet."

"Not yet. But that's not what I wanted to talk to you about."

Annie let him read the two articles about the drowning.

"At least I know the man she was engaged to was Archer Prescott."

"JFP Athletics, huh?"

"Do you know anything about the company or him?"

"I remember when they used to headquarter here in Maine." Ian frowned. "Raised a little bit of a stink when Prescott moved them out to California about ten years ago."

"Peggy mentioned something about that."

"That put most of his employees here out of work, and there was talk that he moved to take advantage of cheaper labor out West. Maybe even illegal labor if he could get away with it, some said. I don't know if there was anything to that, of course." Ian pushed the articles back across the desk to her. "Sounds like he really loved the girl, though. I wonder how long he kept looking for her."

Annie nodded. "I was curious about that too. You know, I was going to let this whole thing drop since I found out she's dead, but I can't quite do it yet. I want to know more. I tried to call Mr. Prescott, but all I could do was leave him a message. If he ever gets it, I doubt he'll call me back. And then there's whoever it is who doesn't want me to find out anything about Susan at all. You don't think there could have been something wrong with the way she died, do you? Something somebody doesn't want me to look into?"

"You mean murder?" Ian shrugged. "Sounds like a pretty straightforward accident to me. I'm sure the authorities looked into it at the time. You have to think about who would have benefited from her death in a case like that. This Prescott guy was pretty well off even then. I can't imagine what Susan might have left him, if she left him anything, would be motive enough for someone that rich."

Annie considered for a minute. "She didn't have any family left that I know of, and I don't think she had money except for what she got from selling the house. As you said, that's just pocket change for someone who owns a manufacturing company like JFP."

"I suppose, if you were bound and determined to find out more than you have already, you could check the court records and see if she left a will that was probated." Ian tapped the side of his nose. "Follow the money, eh?"

"Good idea. Maybe I'll add a trip to the Lincoln County Courthouse to my to-do list."

Once she had left the town hall, Annie walked down to the post office to mail a few of Gram's embroidered aprons back home to LeeAnn. Then she walked back up Main Street to get a few staples from Magruder's Groceries. After that, she went next door to Malone's Hardware.

All the time she was looking at paint chips, she couldn't help wondering about Susan. Why would someone warn her off if there was nothing more to know? And who was that someone?

Finally deciding not to decide, she left the hardware store and went home. She unlocked the front door just as the telephone began to ring.

"Ms. Dawson? This is Lisa Hendrickson from Archer Prescott's office."

"Oh, hello. Thank you for calling me back."

"I'm sorry I don't have better news for you, but I wanted to let you know that Mr. Prescott doesn't speak to reporters unless the interview has been prearranged. He does appreciate your interest."

"But I'm not a reporter, Ms.—excuse me, what was your name?"

"Lisa Hendrickson."

"Ms. Hendrickson. As I said, I'm not a reporter. I'm just an old friend of Susan's, and I'm trying to get some information about her. I've been doing a lot of digging on my own, but there are some things I'd really like to ask Mr. Prescott. I promise I won't take up much of his time. Please tell him that."

Ms. Hendrickson made an impatient little huffing sound. "I'll give him your message, Ms. Dawson, but I can't promise you he'll have the opportunity to return your call. He's very busy, and he's usually pretty firm on matters of this type."

"I understand. But if you'd just tell him what I said, I would appreciate it."

"I'll do that. Good afternoon."

The click on the other end of the phone line was deafening in its finality. This might well be the last dead end.

With a sigh, Annie picked up the decorating book she had left on the coffee table in the living room. If she couldn't find Susan, at least she could make some kind of decision about the upstairs bathroom. She had marked two pages in the book, both with photos of gorgeous bathrooms that would fit in with the rest of the house—bathrooms with wainscoting and claw-foot bathtubs and crown molding. But which one did she like best? The black, red, and cream or the rose and taupe? If she—

The telephone trilled, and she put the book facedown on the sofa beside her. Who could it be now?

"Hello?"

"Is this Ms. Dawson?"

It was a man's voice, deep and warm, a voice she didn't recognize.

"Who's calling, please?"

"This is Archer Prescott. You left a message with my assistant asking me to call."

~9~

masculine chuckle came through the line. "Well, you know how it is, Ms. Dawson. When you're in a position like mine, it's hard to accomplish anything if you don't have someone to weed out some of the calls. Lisa does an excellent job."

"I know you must be very busy, Mr. Prescott, but—"

"Call me Arch. If you were a friend of Susan's, it's only right."

"In that case, it's only right that you call me Annie."

"Fair enough, Annie. Now what can I do for you? Lisa said you have been looking into some things about Susan."

"It's gotten to be a lot more complicated than I thought it was when I started out."

She told him about the letters she had found in the attic, about how she and Susan had met and lost touch, and about what she found out about the drowning.

"That must have been terrible for you."

"It was." Some of the life went out of his voice. "I couldn't believe she was gone."

"The article said you were going to look for her after the accident. Did you find out anything?"

"No. We never did. I had teams of people searching for weeks afterward, but she was gone. It's been more than twenty years now, and I still think of her every day. I wonder if I hadn't left her on deck that night, maybe she ..."

His voice trailed off, and for a moment he was silent. Then he cleared his throat. "Maybe things would have been different. Maybe I didn't deserve someone like her anyway. I don't know."

"I'm so sorry." Annie bit her lip. "I didn't want to stir up any painful memories for you, but I haven't been able to find out much about Susan. I mean, yes, I found out what happened to her, but that doesn't tell me much about how things were for her before she died. Was she happy? Did she ever get to dance on Broadway? She dreamed about that when we were girls."

"That's how I met her." His voice seemed to brighten at the memory. "She was in a show my brother was backing. Just in the chorus line, but I could tell she was special right away. We dated for a while, and I knew she was the girl, you know? I told her right off the bat that we should get married. She thought I was kidding, and maybe I was a little, but if she had said yes, we would have headed straight for the courthouse, no questions asked. Then, when her aunt passed away, I said we should go ahead and take the plunge. No use her trying to get a place of her own and all that when I could take care of her, but she wanted to go home. I guess that's understandable. Her folks were pretty cut up about her Aunt Kim, too, and she wanted to be with them."

"And then they died."

"Yeah." He was silent for another long moment. "Yeah."

"I wish I'd known."

"Poor kid. She didn't have anybody in the world anymore. That's when she decided maybe we ought to get married after all."

"So she lived in Stony Point until that last sailing trip."

"Yeah. Everything happened kind of fast after her parents were killed. I wanted us to have a big wedding, something her folks would have wanted for her, but I didn't want to wait very long either. I had a wedding planner arrange everything down in Vero Beach. That's where my Florida house is. All we had to do was sail down the coast and walk into happily-ever-after. Instead we got the third act of a tragedy."

"I'm really sorry to have brought this all up again."

"No, don't be sorry. It's good to know someone cared enough about Susan to try to find her. And you said you never found out anything else about her? None of your friends knew anything about what happened?"

"No. They all assumed she had married you and moved away somewhere."

"I wish she had. I wish …" He laughed softly. "It'll sound funny, I know, but I've always wondered if she's alive out there somewhere. Maybe she hit her head and lost her memory or something. If you ever find out something that makes you suspect that kind of thing, Annie, you have to let me know. Promise?"

"The Coast Guard seemed pretty certain—"

"I know. Stuff like that doesn't happen in real life. It's been a long, long time too. I mean, I have a wife now and kids and all that, anyway. It's not like Susan and I could get back together or anything. It's just that, if she were out there somewhere, I'd like to know she was taken care of. I guess it's just wishful thinking on my part, but I'd do anything in the world to help her."

"I'm sure you would."

There was silence on the other end of the line again.

Then he cleared his throat.

"Listen, let me give you my cell number. You can call me direct anytime. If there's something I can help you with, or you just want to talk about Susan again, you call me up."

"Oh, I wouldn't dream of bothering you, Mr. Prescott."

"Arch, OK?"

Annie smiled to herself. "Arch."

"And I mean it. If you find out something, or if you want to know anything else about her, even something small, let me know. Susan deserves to be remembered by the people who loved her."

Annie jotted down the telephone number he gave her and soon they said goodbye. Poor man. It was bad enough that he lost the woman he loved, but to carry that guilt all these years had to be terrible for him.

But at least Susan hadn't been entirely alone after her parents died. She had had someone who loved her and who wanted the best for her. Just knowing that made Annie feel so much better. Now if she only knew who wanted her to leave Susan's past buried and forgotten.

*   *   *   *

"You just called him up? In California?"

Annie nodded. "I did."

Kate looked back down at her crochet. "I could never do that. Just call up somebody like that, somebody I don't know. What did he say?"

The ladies of the Hook and Needle Club all paused over their projects. All, that is, except Stella. She did not slow the swift, almost-mechanical *click-click-click* of her knitting needles.

"I met young Prescott when I lived in New York." She pressed her withered lips together. "I didn't like him."

Annie had to hold back a smile. Stella wasn't really as crusty as she seemed sometimes, but it could be difficult to get past her prickliness.

"He was very nice when I talked to him," Annie assured them all. "He still feels bad about not being on deck with Susan that night, even after all these years. And he told me to call him anytime. That's pretty accommodating of someone who owns a big company like that, don't you think?"

"All I remember about Archer Prescott is that he treated Susan like a queen." Mary Beth shook her head. "Jewelry and expensive clothes all the time. I hardly recognized quiet little Susan anymore. She looked more like a runway model or something. The few times she was in town, of course."

"What a life. A handsome rich guy to cater to your every whim. And that on top of being a beautiful blonde." Gwen sighed. "What a life."

Mary Beth sighed too. "I could have used someone like that in my life twenty or thirty years ago."

"It's not too late," Alice insisted. "Mr. Kendall at the bank always seems to perk up when you're in there."

Peggy and Alice exchanged grins, and Mary Beth rolled her eyes.

"Spare me. Mr. Kendall is eighty if he's a day."

Stella stopped knitting and looked up. "Anything wrong with eighty?" She narrowed her eyes at Mary Beth and then the tiniest hint of a smile crept into her expression.

"Besides, I happen to know Aaron Kendall is just a young pup of seventy-six."

Annie laughed. "Maybe he's holding off courting you until after you get the shop all spruced up, Mary Beth. Did you ever get things set up for Tom Maxwell to put your cabinets in for you?"

"Ugh. You know, every time I think that company has it right, they find something else to mess up. I looked inside one of the boxes, and the units they sent don't have the dividers I wanted. They have promised me they'll have the right ones in by the end of this week. Absolutely." Mary Beth shrugged. "But they gave me free shipping to make up for some of the hassle, so I guess it's not all bad."

Peggy knotted her dark olive thread and began appliquéing another leaf on her quilt block. "I gave you Tom's number, didn't I? Of course, Wally will be glad to do it for you sometime after Christmas."

"I don't think I can wait quite that long, as much as I'd like to. But, yes, you did give me the number. If I ever get the right cabinets in here with all the right accessories, I'll definitely call him."

The mention of Tom Maxwell reminded Annie of her desire to see Susan's old house again, which reminded her about checking into Susan's will. It was a pretty afternoon, cold but sunny. Maybe this would be a good day to head up to the courthouse in Wiscasset. It was only about thirty miles away.

* * * *

The Last Will and Testament of Susan Alexandria Morris

was, for a legal document, relatively short and straightforward. It stated her place of residence as Lincoln County, Maine, and named Archer Lee Prescott as her executor. The crux of the whole document was contained in Article II, Section 1:

I give, devise and bequeath all of my property which I may own at the time of my death, real, personal and mixed, tangible and intangible, of whatsoever nature and wheresoever situated, including all property which I may acquire or be entitled to after execution of this Will, to Archer Lee Prescott, to be his absolutely, if he survives me.

The property bequeathed to Archer Lee Prescott was listed on the inventory filed with the court. It consisted of cash, doubtless from the sale of the Morris home a month before Susan's death, and a few personal effects. All in all, her estate was nothing that would entice a wealthy man like Prescott to do anything underhanded. Everything Annie had seen in the court records indicated that he had fulfilled his duties as executor promptly and faithfully. Following the money had led to another dead end.

So what was it that made someone so determined to keep Annie from finding out what happened to Susan?

She thought about it during the drive home from Wiscasset. When she reached Stony Point, she turned onto Main Street and pulled up in front of the town hall. Thank goodness Chief Edwards was on duty at the front desk today. She didn't want to have to go through Roy to get to him, and she didn't want to have to ask Roy any favors, either.

"Mrs. Dawson, good to see you." Edwards offered her a

chair. "What can I do for you today?"

"I think just about everybody in town has heard by now that Susan Morris, the woman I was looking for, is dead."

Edwards nodded. "I did hear that. I'm sorry."

Annie hesitated for a moment. "Do you think you could look into something for me? I've been checking some of the newspapers and public records, trying to get information about Susan. I found out she drowned at a place called Folly Beach in South Carolina in August 1989. Is there any chance you could find out what's in the records there about Susan? I know you're busy and everything, but I was just thinking …"

She ended with a hopeful lift of her eyebrows.

"It's not technically police business since we'd have no reason to reopen the case, but let me see what I can find out for you. You said Folly Beach, South Carolina, in August of 1989?"

Annie nodded, and Chief Edwards wrote the information down on the yellow legal pad on his desk.

"Something that long ago may take a little while to hear back on, but I'll give it a try."

"That would be wonderful. Thank you."

"I'm not making any guarantees, you realize."

"I know that, but if you can find out something, anything at all." Annie exhaled. "I can't help thinking there must be more to know. Why else would someone want to warn me to stay out of Susan's business?"

The chief's face was grave. "There is that. And I'm sorry we don't have an answer to that particular question yet."

Annie smiled. "There's not much to go on, is there?"

"No, but we'll keep our eyes open, don't you worry. And on this Charleston matter, I'll let you know if I find out anything."

~ 10 ~

When Annie got home, she got out her recipe book and the ingredients for chocolate-chip cookies. Baking was such a soothingly ordinary task, and the twins would definitely enjoy a special surprise from Grammy. While she was in the middle of making the dough, her telephone rang.

"Sorry it's taken me a while to get back to you about Tom Maxwell working on the cabinets," Mary Beth said. "With one thing and another, I've been really busy. Today I marked down the embroidery floss, and it's flying off the shelves."

"You're not putting your wool yarns on sale anytime soon, are you?"

"I'll make sure you're the first to know. Now, do you want the good news or the bad news?"

Annie wedged the phone between her shoulder and the side of her head and went back to mixing cookie dough. "Hmm, if there's bad news, you'd better sweeten it with the good stuff first."

"I finally got the right cabinets in. I made the delivery guy stand there while I opened every one of the boxes and made sure they had sent what I ordered."

Annie chuckled.

"And I talked to Tom Maxwell. He can do my cabinets, and his rates aren't bad at all."

"Great. I want to find out if his wife is all right and then drop the whole thing."

"OK," Mary Beth said, "but you'll have to be patient until next week."

"Next week?"

"That's the bad news. Tom won't be able to come until Monday. But it will probably take a day or two for him to get everything assembled and installed, so that'll give you plenty of time to talk to his wife while he's occupied."

"OK, I guess that'll have to do. Hang on. I need to put in some chocolate chips." Annie put down the phone, added the semisweet morsels she had measured out, and then put the phone back to her ear. "Anyway, I guess if Sandy Maxwell's been OK for this long, a few more days won't make a big difference."

"I'm sorry you didn't have better news about Susan," Mary Beth said, "but I see that hasn't discouraged your sleuthing tendencies."

"Ah, well, I guess we don't always get happy endings, but at least I know what happened. And this thing with Sandy Maxwell isn't a real mystery or anything. Just a neighbor checking on a neighbor. That can't be a bad thing, can it?"

"Annie, you're a sweetheart. And I bet you're baking something to give to somebody else."

Annie laughed and started stirring again. "Just some chocolate-chip cookies to send down to the grandkids. My daughter's been hinting pretty hard that I need to come back home. I figured a special delivery of some of my home-made cookies should appease the little ones at least for a while. I'm sending some more of Gram's fancy work down to LeeAnn too."

"I'd be pretty homesick for them if it was me," Mary Beth admitted. "All I have is my niece, Amy, and I really miss her between visits. Well, there's my sister, of course, but, um, we're working on that particular relationship."

"Have you talked to her much since your mother passed away?"

"A couple of times." There was regret in Mary Beth's voice. "She stays pretty busy."

"How's Amy?"

"She's doing fine. She and this young man she works with seem to have hit it off."

"Is that Elliot? Umm, Evan?"

"Everett."

"That's right. The one with the little boy. Just think, soon you could be a step-great-aunt."

Mary Beth chuckled. "I'll leave that to Amy for now, but his son Peter is a sweet little fellow. And at least I'd have something to show when all you grandmas whip out the photos."

A maidenly little *ding* from the oven timer brought Annie back to matters at hand.

"Listen, Mary Beth, my oven's hot now. I have to put these cookies in. We'll plan on Monday unless I hear from you."

"Sure thing. Happy baking."

Annie hung up the phone and started spooning out dough. Soon she had two dozen cookies plumping up in the oven, and two dozen more ready to go in next.

While the cookies baked, she washed out the mixing

bowl and spoon she had used. Then she laid out a generous length of waxed paper, ready for when the cookies came out of the oven. Gram had taught her the little trick of moistening the countertop to make the paper lie flat instead of curling up. It was just a little thing, but it made using the waxed paper so much easier.

There had to be some things, some little things, she could do to make it easier to get to know Sandy Maxwell. Annie still felt foolish when she remembered her so-called conversation with Tom. No wonder he hadn't been very receptive.

Maybe, once she had made sure things at the Maxwells' were OK, she and Sandy could become friends. And then maybe that would make it easier to get to know Tom too. Annie knew too well how hard it could be to find a place to fit in a small town like Stony Point where everybody knew everybody else and their business. Maybe nobody had ever reached out to the Maxwells before now. She couldn't imagine how lonely it must be to live out there away from everybody.

By the time the last of the cookies had cooled, Annie had decided that the Maxwells were much too isolated. A few chocolate-chip cookies and some good, old-fashioned neighborliness might just be the cure.

*　　*　　*　　*

"I'm still not too sure about this." Alice looked up at Tom and Sandy Maxwell's house. "I'd feel a lot better if there were some neighbors around."

"We *are* around." Annie turned off the engine and

unbuckled her seatbelt. "Besides, you were the one who insisted on coming along. I could have done this by myself."

Alice scurried out of the passenger seat with Annie's bag of cookies. "No, I told you I was coming, and I meant it. We're here now, so we'd better make the most of it." She considered for a moment. "Do you suppose she could use some new costume jewelry or some reasonably priced home decor?"

Annie shook her head, chuckling. "You are *not* going to try to sell her anything."

"Of course not." Alice grinned. "Not right away. But if we're trying to get her to meet people, what could be better than a party? And if there just happens to be jewelry or decorative items available, well …"

She shrugged, and Annie hurried her up to the house. "You know you're not serious. Just behave." She used the brass knocker. They waited for several minutes, but no one came to the door. "Well, we know Tom is at A Stitch in Time, but Sandy's got to be here."

Alice shook her head. "Waste of a trip, if you ask me."

Annie knocked again, and the sound seemed loud inside the apparently empty house. "You stay here in case she comes to the door. I'm going to look around a little bit." She went down the steps and made her way around to the side of the house, answering Alice's protests with just a smile and a little wave.

Someone here certainly loved the garden. Even though it was all falling asleep in preparation for winter, it was obvious that the grounds were carefully tended. Here in the back, the daylilies, phlox, lupines, bleeding hearts, and all the others must make a perfect riot of glorious color come springtime.

Annie wandered down the flagstone path, admiring the well-maintained trees and shrubs, and the picturesque layout of the garden. It hadn't been this way when she was here with Susan. At least she didn't remember it this way. Susan had had a little patch of flowers that she enjoyed looking after. In fact, she had been quite particular about keeping it just so, but her parents had been too busy to do much more than keep their yard presentable. Susan would have liked it the way it was now.

The yard was very large, stretching back to the woods and the creek that lay beyond. Annie drifted toward the farthest part of it, toward the little plot that was surrounded by a wrought-iron fence. She remembered that fence, black and rusted in places, each picket with a spike finial on the end of it, discouraging climbing. It wasn't a high fence, but it was enough. She and Susan hadn't been brave enough to explore the little family cemetery back when they were girls.

Annie unlatched the gate and opened it, smiling at the protesting shriek it made. There was no doubt that, thirty years ago, the sound would have been enough to send her and Susan both scurrying back to the house with shrieks that were only half in fun.

She scanned the markers, picking out dates, calculating the ages of those who had died. *Eli Morris, 1811.* That was the oldest one she saw. There wasn't another date to tell her when this Eli Morris had been born, so she didn't know if he had died old or young, but there were others in both categories among the dozen or so graves. Most of them had been Morrises, but she also saw headstones marked Stanley and Childress and Marquette. It wasn't a large plot, just enough to be shaded by a pair of large maple trees, but there was something stately and serene about it.

Most of the burials seemed to have been in the nineteenth century or very early in the twentieth, but there was one from 1955, obviously the widow of a man who had passed away in 1908, and who had finally been laid to rest at his side. At the farthest corner of the enclosure, Annie noticed one large stone that was newer than the rest. It was dated 1989.

Ellen Patricia and Jack Lawson Morris.

Susan's parents were buried here. Too bad there wasn't a marker for Susan herself. Annie decided that, if she ever called him again, she'd ask Archer Prescott if there was a memorial for Susan somewhere. Maybe he had arranged something. Someone should have.

With a sigh, she went back to the iron gate. Alice would have search parties out looking for her if she didn't get back to business pretty soon. Just as she lifted the latch, she caught a flicker of movement out of the corner of her eye. Someone was over in the trees between her and the house. She could see a hint of pink and yellow behind the greens and browns.

"Hello?"

There was no reply, and Annie took a few quick steps forward.

"Hello? Mrs. Maxwell?"

For another moment, there was only silent stillness; then a woman stepped out of the trees and onto the flagstone path. Her dark hair was gathered into a short little ponytail, and she wore a gardening smock covered with roses, bright pink and yellow.

"Did you want something?"

She put up her hand, shading her eyes from the sun, not moving any closer.

Annie came up to her. "You *are* Sandy Maxwell, aren't you?"

She seemed to be about Annie's age, but she was taller and slimmer. With the sun the way it was, Annie couldn't really tell what color her eyes were, but there was a certain undeniable anxiousness in them.

"Did you want something?" she asked again. "Tom's not here right now, but if you need some handyman work done, I can give him the message."

Annie smiled. "Actually, I came to see you. I was by here the other day and spoke to your husband."

"Was that you? Yes, he mentioned it to me. I hope he wasn't too gruff with you. He doesn't mean to be. We really don't get into town much, though. I'm sure he told you."

"He did, but I still thought I'd come out and meet you. I haven't been in Stony Point long, and I thought I'd just get to know everybody."

There was something wistful in Mrs. Maxwell's eyes, but she shook her head. "Tom and I really don't—"

"Hey, there! Did you forget about me?" Alice hurried up to them. "You must be Mrs. Maxwell."

Annie took her arm, drawing her closer. "This is Alice McFarlane. I'm sorry, but I never did introduce myself. I'm Annie Dawson."

"Oh, um, yes. I'm sure that's the name Tom mentioned to me. I'm sorry he wasn't very welcoming that day, but we don't get a lot of visitors, and he'd been napping." Mrs. Maxwell smiled uncertainly. "He's a good man. Really."

"Wally says he does a good job."

"Wally?"

"Wally Carson," Annie said. "He does most of the odd jobs around Stony Point, but he said if he was busy that we couldn't go wrong with Tom Maxwell."

Mrs. Maxwell ducked her head, but there was a pleased expression on her face. "That's nice of him. I think Tom's mentioned him, too, come to think of it."

"You must be quite a gardener." Annie glanced around the yard again, imagining what it would be like in the spring. "I bet it's really pretty come April or May. It's certainly different than it was when I used to come here."

Again Mrs. Maxwell looked shyly pleased.

"I've made a lot of changes since we moved in. The people who lived here before Tom and me didn't do anything much at all with the yard."

"It's nice. And I've always liked the house. I love how solid it is, as if it's been here forever and always will be."

Mrs. Maxwell smiled a little, and Annie could see now that her eyes were dark blue.

"I've always liked it too. I mean, ever since we've been here. It's a real home, not just a place to live."

"That's what my friend used to say about it," Annie said.

"I always loved visiting."

Mrs. Maxwell's smile faded, and again she shaded her eyes with one hand. "Tom said you knew someone who used to live here."

"Susan Morris. Her parents are buried over in your cemetery."

"Yes."

"You must take care of their graves, of all the graves, for them to look so neat."

Mrs. Maxwell turned toward the little fenced-in area. "It just seemed right, you know. I guess most of those people lived in the house at one time or other. Someone should look after them."

"And the house, too, right?"

"The house too."

"I wonder how much it's changed since Susan lived here. She always loved the place."

Annie waited, but Mrs. Maxwell made no reply. She didn't even turn to face them again.

"I guess gardening takes up a lot of your time," Alice ventured. "Annie and I both do a lot of crafts, crochet and cross-stitch, and that kind of thing. Do you have any hobbies?"

Mrs. Maxwell finally turned around, but she kept her eyes on the dormant grass at her feet.

"No, I really don't do any of that. By the time I've done the gardening and the housework, I really don't—"

"Sandy?"

Mrs. Maxwell's head jerked up, and her eyes got big. "I—I really have to go now."

"Sandy?" Tom Maxwell came around the side of the house, his large work boots eating up the ground between them in short order. He glanced at Annie and Alice, and then at his wife. "I didn't know you had company, honey."

She shrugged a little, and her lips trembled into an uncertain smile. "I was working in the garden, and they just dropped by."

"We thought we'd take just a minute to introduce ourselves. I know I came at a bad time the other day, but Alice and I—" Annie pulled Alice a little closer to her. "This is Alice McFarlane. She lives next door to me over on Ocean Drive. Anyway, we were just saying that—"

"Look, Mrs. Dawson. That *is* your name, right?"

Annie nodded.

"Mrs. Dawson, I told you before, my wife and I don't do much socializing. I'm sure you and your friend mean well, but we like our privacy." Tom Maxwell fixed his dark eyes on them. "You can understand that, can't you?"

Annie bit her lip and nodded.

He put his arm around his wife's slender shoulders. "We like our privacy, don't we, honey?"

Mrs. Maxwell glanced at Annie and then looked away. "I don't do any of that needlework stuff you were talking about, Mrs. Dawson. My garden keeps me pretty busy anyway. But thanks for stopping by."

Her husband squeezed her closer to him. "Is there anything else we can do for you ladies?"

Annie shook her head. "We just wanted to introduce ourselves."

"Let us know if you decide you want company." Alice

handed Mrs. Maxwell the bag of cookies. "Annie thought you might like a homemade treat."

Mr. Maxwell took the bag from his wife, his expression more wary than appreciative.

"We're fine on our own."

～ 44 ～

*I*t wasn't until Annie had backed her car down the long driveway and turned into the street that she or Alice said anything.

"That was weird." Alice's eyes widened. "Aren't you glad you didn't go by yourself?"

Annie grinned. "And you didn't even see the graveyard."

"I can't imagine living by a graveyard."

"It's only a little one."

"Stop it." Alice pulled her jacket a little more snugly around herself. "Besides, it wasn't that kind of weird. Still, I don't know about him. She seemed kind of jumpy when he showed up."

"Yeah, obviously. He about scared the life out of me, that's for sure. I thought Mary Beth would keep him busy with her cabinets at least for the whole day."

"She did say that was scheduled for today, didn't she?"

"Definitely." Annie took a deep calming breath. "OK. No big deal. He didn't chase us off with a shotgun or anything."

"At least I gave her my business card. As my friend Rachel from Brooklyn says, 'so it shouldn't be a total loss.' "

"You did?"

Alice grinned. "In the bag of cookies."

"You just had to get in some kind of sales pitch, didn't you?"

"Seriously, I just wanted her to have some way to get in touch with us if she decides she wants to. I see what you mean about things being strange with her and her husband."

"I did expect him to be busy all day." Annie frowned. "At least Mary Beth could have warned us or something." She tossed her purse to Alice. "Where is my phone? I'm surprised she didn't call me. She has my cell number."

"I don't see it here." Alice then dug through her own bag and pulled out her phone. "She might have called my phone. Uh-oh, it wasn't on. Sorry." She punched a few buttons and then held it to her ear. From her side of the car, Annie could hear the tinny message it played. "Alice, this is Mary Beth. I tried to reach Annie at her house, but didn't get an answer. I hope you two haven't gone yet. Tom Maxwell left the shop. He might be on his way home. Call me."

"Great." Annie sighed. "So much for the cunning plan. What did I do with my phone? I'm sure I put it in my bag."

At the next red light, she started rummaging around under the car seat. Finally she came up with three quarters, a note reminding her to buy sunscreen, and her cell phone.

"A lot of good you did me today," she muttered before returning it to her purse.

"At least we got to talk to Mrs. Maxwell," Alice said, "so that much was a success. And even if things did feel sort of tense out there, she looked all right. She seemed healthy and everything."

"She seemed scared. I hope she didn't get into trouble for talking to us."

"If she needed help, she would have said something before he got there." Alice's forehead wrinkled. "Wouldn't she?"

"I hope she would."

When they got back to Main Street, Annie pulled up in front of A Stitch in Time. When she and Alice came inside, Mary Beth hurried from behind the counter.

"I'm glad you're here. I tried to call you both. Didn't you get my message?"

Alice shrugged one shoulder. "I'm afraid I forgot to turn my phone on, and Annie's fell out of her purse in the car. What happened, anyway? I thought it would take him a while to put those cabinets together and then install them. He's not done already, is he?"

Mary Beth pressed her lips together, and her eyes narrowed. "He hadn't been working down there very long before he came up to tell me that all the screws are missing from the boxes. He can't really get started on anything until the replacements get here."

"Can't you just get some more from the hardware store?"

"Evidently they're a special kind made just for this company." Mary Beth took a deep breath and then smiled. "It would be funny if it weren't so irritating. I don't know how one outfit could manage to do something wrong every single time I talk to them."

Annie patted her arm. "I'm sorry, Mary Beth."

"Oh well. There can only be so many things that can get messed up, right? It has to all work out eventually. Good thing you two came here before you did anything else. I was afraid you would be out at the Maxwells, and Tom would find you there."

Annie grinned ruefully. "That's exactly what did happen."

"Uh-oh. Is everything OK out there?"

"I'm not sure. His wife didn't come to the door, and when I went around to the backyard, she was standing in the trees where I couldn't see her."

"That's strange. She's not, um … different, is she?" Mary Beth asked. "I mean, poor thing, maybe she just has issues."

Annie shook her head. "No, she seemed perfectly rational to me. But she was nervous about something. Didn't you think so, Alice?"

"Yeah. Mostly about her husband showing up."

"That did seem to make things worse." Annie considered for a minute. "I wonder if anybody in town is actually friends with him. Maybe I should talk to Wally, since they've worked together and everything."

"That's a good idea," Mary Beth said. "Though you know how men are. They can be friends for years and not know a thing about each other."

Alice made a face. "And good luck getting one of them to talk."

Annie laughed. "Now, now, you both know that's not fair. My Wayne wasn't that way at all. And every time I've been around Ian, he's been very nice to talk to."

Alice and Mary Beth exchanged knowing glances, and Annie rolled her eyes.

"Cut it out, you two. You know Ian and I are just friends."

Alice chuckled. "That's not his fault."

"Just stop." Annie turned to Mary Beth. "So when are the new screws for your cabinets supposed to get here?"

Mary Beth sighed. "They don't know. Evidently there's

a problem with them at the factory, and they have to be redesigned or something."

"But then you'll have Tom come back, right?"

Alice's eyebrows shot up to her hairline. "You're not going back out there!"

"I didn't get a chance to talk to Sandy. Not really."

"Annie ..."

"You saw her. Something is worrying her."

"Maybe that something is just none of our business. Did you ever think of that? Maybe her mother is sick, or she had an argument with her sister or something. Maybe her flower beds have grub worms, or her toilet's stopped up."

"Her husband would fix that." Annie grinned. "When he had time."

"Look, he made it very clear that they don't like visitors. Maybe we should just respect that."

Annie put her hands up in surrender. "OK. OK."

For now.

*   *   *   *

"Mom, please be careful."

Over the telephone, Annie could hear the concern in LeeAnn's voice and could easily picture it on her face.

"Nothing's going to happen to me, honey. Just because Mr. Maxwell likes his privacy, that doesn't mean he's dangerous. It's been three days since I went out there, and I'm still in one piece."

"I don't think I like you up there snooping around by yourself."

"You just don't like me up here at all." Annie bit her tongue and managed a more playful tone. "The boogeyman isn't going to get me, you know."

"Mom."

It was LeeAnn's "now that Dad's gone, you need somebody to take care of you" voice. Annie appreciated the love behind it, even if it was sometimes confining.

"Honey, I'm a big girl now. I can look after myself."

"I know, but there are some weird people out there. You should know that better than anybody."

"And I have a lot of good friends up here too. We all take care of each other and help when we need to. It's only right that I try to help Mrs. Maxwell if I can."

"If she's in trouble, maybe you should tell the police."

"But I don't know that, honey. And getting somebody's husband in trouble with the law isn't usually the best way to make friends."

"Mom, if they don't want you to come around there, and you don't think she's actually in trouble, maybe you should just leave them alone, huh?"

Maybe LeeAnn was right, but she hadn't seen Sandy Maxwell's face. Behind the uneasiness, the woman had seemed hungry for a little companionship. If she and her husband had lived out there for almost a decade, keeping to themselves all that time, she must be dying to talk to someone, woman to woman, at least once in a while.

"We'll see what happens," Annie replied. "But you don't need to worry about it."

LeeAnn exhaled audibly. "OK. You're coming home for Herb's birthday though, right?"

"Did you get the package I sent?"

"Yeah, it came a couple of days ago."

"You didn't open it, did you?"

"No. What is it?"

"What it is … is a surprise!" Annie waited for a moment. "OK?"

"OK. I wasn't going to tell him, you know. So are you coming or not? The party's on the tenth. You could come a few days before and stay until the Monday after Thanksgiving."

"That's a pretty long time. I was thinking I'd come a day or two before Thanksgiving and leave a couple of days after. How's that?"

"Herb's going to be pretty disappointed."

Annie laughed. "Who all is coming to the party?"

"Everybody. Herb's family and ours, and some neighbors and a lot of the people from church and from his office."

"It sounds like he'll be so busy with all his guests that he won't miss me at all."

"But I miss you, Mom. The twins miss you."

Annie wished she could reach out and hug her daughter right through the phone. "I know, sweetie, and I miss you all. You don't realize how much. But I still have a lot to do up here, and it's just not practical for me to be coming back there all the time. It would be better for me to get this done once and for all, right?"

"I suppose. It just seems like it never gets done. I mean, you did all that research to find out what happened to your friend Susan, and then the minute you know, you're totally obsessed with these Maxwell people. I just don't like it."

Annie could picture the pout that went with her daughter's tone of voice.

"I promise I'll come for Thanksgiving, and we'll cook up the greatest meal ever, OK?"

"OK, Mom."

"And I'll spend the rest of the time spoiling my grandbabies."

LeeAnn chuckled. "You do enough of that long distance."

"In the meantime, you make sure to tell Herb I wished him a happy birthday, and that I hope he likes the present I sent him. But he can't have it before his birthday!"

"Don't worry," LeeAnn assured her. "He doesn't even know you sent him anything yet."

"Good. That way he won't be nosing around for hints. Now you'd better let me go so I can get back to work."

"All right, Mom. Talk to you later."

"Give the twins a big hug for me."

"I will. And Mom?"

"Yes?"

"Be careful."

Once she had hung up, Annie sat for a moment, just staring at the telephone. LeeAnn and the kids were so far away. She missed her church and her friends in Texas too. And she missed the home she and Wayne had shared. Yes, it was painful to be there and feel so keenly his absence, but it held his memory too, and it had been her home for so long.

But Gram's memory was here at Grey Gables along with all the memories of Annie's childhood summers. And Alice was here, and Mary Beth and all the Hook and Needle Club ladies, and all the friends from her new church. And—

Annie felt a furry little muzzle poke itself into her hand.

"And you, Miss Boots." She pulled the cat into a snug embrace. "For now, we're just going to enjoy ourselves. We're going to get the house fixed up and sort through Gram's things and have fun with our friends. And we're going to try our best to be friends with Sandy Maxwell, too, because everybody should have a friend."

The thirty-year-old memory of lonely little Susan Morris standing on the beach watching the other children play came back to Annie's mind, and she held the purring cat closer.

"Everybody should have a friend."

The telephone beside her rang, and she put the cat down on the couch. She picked up the receiver. "Hello?"

"Hi, Annie. This is Clara Robbins. I just wanted to remind you about the meeting we're having on Thursday to plan the harvest banquet. I hope you'll be able to join us."

"I'll sure try, Clara."

"Oh, and mum's the word, but the banquet is also going to be a surprise party for Reverend Wallace's 25th anniversary with the church. We want it to be extra special."

Reverend Wallace. Of course!

"That's wonderful, Clara. I'll definitely be there. See you soon."

Annie hung up, unable to keep from smiling. Why hadn't she thought of Reverend Wallace before now? He might remember Susan, and he might have some good advice about what to do about Sandy Maxwell. Annie had to go into town to order some new checks, anyway, so she might as well take care of that tomorrow.

It was just a short walk from the bank to the church.

～ 12 ～

"Mrs. Dawson! Good morning! Annie turned to see Reverend Wallace standing under one of the enormous oaks that, in the summertime, shaded the church grounds. He was leaning on a rake beside an impressive pile of red and brown leaves.

"Good morning, Reverend Wallace." She hurried over to him. "Just the man I wanted to see."

"That's what I like to hear. And what can I do for you today?"

"To tell you the truth, I'm not really sure if there's anything you can do. I happened to be out at Tom Maxwell's house a while ago, and I was wondering how well you know him and his wife."

"Not very well. I've called on them a couple of times and told them both we'd love to have them here at Stony Point Community, but he said they do their worship in private. He was polite enough, but didn't give me much chance to offer more than a standing invitation."

"Yes, he told me he'd met you." Annie smiled at him. "He said you're a nice guy."

He winked at her. "Word's getting out. But seriously, I don't know much about either of them. He told me they keep to themselves mostly, and that seems to be exactly what they do."

"That's what he told me too. Anyway, I wanted to ask you about Sandy."

"Mrs. Maxwell?" He took a handkerchief from his back pocket, mopped his face and the balding top of his head, and then gestured to a nearby stone bench. "My old hip is acting up again."

"You should have some of the boys out here doing this." Annie sat next to him. "Couldn't the youth group—"

"Oh, they do. Year-round, they do a wonderful job of keeping the grounds tidy. And our men's group helps out as well—regular as clockwork." He smiled ruefully. "And sometimes I think I'm twenty years younger than I am and try to do their jobs for them."

Annie returned that smile that twinkled in his eyes. "And do you let them preach your sermons for you?"

He chuckled. "Point taken, but I couldn't help myself. When God makes a day like this, it seems like a sin not to go out and enjoy it."

Annie breathed in as much of the cold, clean air as she could hold and then let it out again. "It's wonderful, isn't it? It reminds me of when I was out at the Maxwells'. They have a wonderful garden, even this time of year. That seems to be Sandy's main hobby."

"Yes, she did mention that when I met her. It was about all she said."

"That's exactly what worries me. She's so isolated out there, and she seems a little, well, a little scared. OK, maybe *scared* isn't quite the word, but she does seem anxious about something. And it only got worse when her husband came home unexpectedly and found me and Alice McFarlane there."

"Oh my. He didn't threaten you, did he?"

"No, nothing like that, but I could tell it made Sandy more nervous than she was before. I just don't know if I should be concerned about her or not. She seemed healthy enough and everything. Alice says maybe we were just there at a bad time."

"That's possible, of course. I've had to remind myself of the very same thing when I make calls sometimes. Despite my best efforts, I don't always manage to show up at the most convenient moment. Did you go to see the Maxwells for a reason?"

"I wanted to see where my friend Susan used to live."

"Ah, the one you've been asking about."

Annie laughed. "I think everybody in town knows that by now, thanks to Peggy Carson."

"Peggy means well," he said, his brown eyes twinkling.

"Oh, I know she does. It's nice of her to ask around too. Working at The Cup & Saucer, she comes in contact with a lot more people than I do. I guess you knew Susan, right?"

"Not really. Not well, anyway. She had been at school when I first came to Stony Point and had just come back here to live when her parents passed away. She was … she was different after that." A sadness came into his eyes. "No, I take that back. She was different before that. I realize New York is a big place, and it's not surprising that a young woman might leave behind some of her small-town ways. And after all, I had not known that much about her in the first place, except what her mother and father happened to mention from time to time. But from what I had seen of her, she had always been rather quiet, maybe a little shy."

Annie nodded. "I always thought so. I could never imagine her being on the stage on Broadway in front of huge audiences, but I guess some people are like that, singers and actors and dancers. They can do anything as long as they get to be someone else while they're doing it."

Reverend Wallace smiled. "Every now and then, I get a little tongue-tied myself one-on-one, but I feel perfectly at home behind the pulpit. I can see Susan being that way."

"But you said she was different when she came back here to live. What do you mean?"

He shrugged. "Just not quite the girl I remembered. She seemed very concerned with her clothing and with her status, and not very friendly with the people here in town."

"That doesn't sound much like the Susan I knew. But she had been on Broadway after I knew her, and her Aunt Kim worked for a fashion magazine. I guess it's a whole different world when you're always rubbing elbows with the rich and famous. Oh, and I found out that Susan's aunt died just a short while before her parents did. Did you know about that at the time?"

"I seem to remember something like that. I guess that could explain some of it, though she seemed more distant than sad, if you ask me. Her mother asked me to talk to her. She said she had been worried about Susan and couldn't get her to say much of anything. But it was no use. Susan wouldn't talk to me, either."

"Did her mother say why she was worried about her?"

"Not specifically. Of course, she was thinking of getting married at the time, and it could have been just uncertainty about making that kind of a commitment.

It's hard to say." Again there was a twinkle in his eyes. "Especially since twenty years have passed since then."

"Did you ever meet her fiancé, Archer Prescott?"

"Only once. He came to talk to me about having the wedding in the church. He seemed eager to have it here with Susan's family and everything, but then she told me she hadn't decided what she wanted to do. Neither of them talked to me about it again, but I got the impression that our little church wasn't quite the venue she was looking for. I understand they had decided to have a big wedding out of state."

"That was the plan." Annie couldn't help feeling sorry that Susan and her Prince Charming had never made it to the altar. "I wish I knew what was going on with her back then. I wish I had stayed in touch with her, especially after her mom and dad were gone."

"I think she left Stony Point rather soon after that. A few weeks, I think. I never spoke to her again once the funeral was over. I tried to, but she never returned my calls."

"Poor Susan, it must have been hard for her. You don't—" Annie bit her lip, not liking the thought that came into her mind. "You don't think she might have drowned herself on purpose, do you?"

"I don't know. I suppose it's possible, but I couldn't say that from the limited contact I had with her."

"But with all her family gone so suddenly, maybe she was overwhelmed and didn't know what she was doing."

"And yet she was getting married and marrying a man of considerable wealth and position. Besides all the material things, from everything I heard, he would have done anything for her, and she was swept off her feet by him. It's what every young woman dreams of. Or so I'm told."

Annie exhaled. "That's what I heard too. It seems such a shame."

"I'm sorry I can't be more help to you about Susan. It's been a long while, and the old memory isn't what it used to be. Still, let's not miss the opportunity to help those who are with us now. If you think Mrs. Maxwell is in trouble, I can contact the authorities for you. No one need know that you said anything at all."

Annie shook her head. "I just don't think it's as serious as that. I'd like to talk to her again."

"I should have stayed in touch with her." Reverend Wallace kicked at a bright yellow leaf that had blown against the bench. "Of course, some women in bad situations never admit they're in trouble."

"That's what I'm afraid of. I'll definitely try to talk to her again."

"And let me know if there's anything you want me to do. I'll be more than happy to go with you, if you'd like."

"No, I don't want her to feel like we're ganging up on her. Let me just go over and have a chat with her, woman to woman." Annie stood up and pulled her coat more closely around herself. "The best thing you can do is pray that everything is all right and that I will know what to do if it's not."

Reverend Wallace stood, too, and gave her hand a warm little squeeze. "I'll certainly do that. You let me know if I can help."

*   *   *   *

Annie ducked her head against the wind as she walked back to the bank to get her car. It seemed colder all of a sudden.

Of course, some women never admit it when they're in trouble. Was that true of Sandy Maxwell? Had it been true of Susan too? No one had ever suggested that Susan's death might be suicide, but it was possible, wasn't it? Wasn't it possible that, behind the facade of a fashion-conscious sophisticate, she had been desperately lonely? That she had been grieving for her aunt and her parents, and had never admitted it to anyone? Not even to Archer Prescott?

Surely he would have said something if he suspected she had taken her own life. Or maybe the thought was too painful for him to face. She hated to bring it up to him. Obviously, the memory of Susan's death was still a difficult one. If she—

"Annie!"

Annie turned to see Mary Beth hurrying toward her. "Hi!"

"Do you have your cell phone with you today?"

Annie wrinkled her forehead. "In my purse. Why?"

"I got those new screws for my cabinets, and Tom Maxwell's at the shop putting them in right now. He should be busy for the rest of the day, but I want to make sure I can call you if he leaves for some reason."

Annie grinned and grabbed her phone. "OK. It's charged and turned on. I'm going to run out and talk to Sandy Maxwell, if she'll let me. But you've absolutely got to let me know if Tom leaves the shop—deal?"

"Deal. Are you sure you shouldn't take Alice with you? Or Ian?"

"As long as you keep an eye on Tom, I'll be fine. Besides, if I wait to get Alice in on this, I might miss my opportunity."

"OK. You keep your phone on and with you, and I'll watch things here. And you call me when you're on the way back."

Mary Beth shook a cautioning finger at her, and Annie couldn't hold back a smile.

"I promise. Now you'd better let me get going before Tom decides he needs a monkey wrench or something from home."

"Scoot, then. I should get back before he wonders where I am."

"Kate's there, isn't she?"

"Yes, but I don't like to leave her there alone." There was reluctant concern in Mary Beth's eyes. "Just in case."

"We'd better both get going." Annie got into her car and started the engine. "I'll let you know how it goes. Do you want me to drop you back at the shop?"

"Better not. If he sees you, he might think something suspicious is going on. It's just a few doors down. Hurry up now."

The bank was on the corner of Main and Elm, so all Annie had to do was drive around the corner and head straight to the Maxwells' home. A few minutes later she had the house in sight, and she was in luck. Sandy was out front getting a package and some letters from the mailbox.

When she saw Annie, she glanced back toward the house as if she was deciding whether or not she could disappear into it. But Annie was quick to pull up beside her.

"Hello there. I hope you'll forgive me for dropping by

again, but we never really did get a chance to talk. Do you have a few minutes?"

Sandy glanced toward the house again. "I shouldn't really—"

"Just for a minute." Annie smiled encouragingly. "I promise I don't bite."

She could feel the wind whip through the trees and noticed Sandy pulling her jacket closer to her neck.

"I bet it's warmer in the house than it is out here."

"Yeah." Sandy's expression softened just the tiniest bit. "You'd better come in."

Annie pulled up in the drive and got out of the car. "Brr. It wasn't bad outside just a little while ago, but now I'm wondering if we're going to get some more snow."

"Maybe you'd better not stay long if the weather is getting bad."

Annie scurried into the house behind her reluctant hostess. "I won't."

Sandy showed her into the small sitting room at the front of the house. It was cozy, warmed with a bright fire in the hearth and furnishings from the early 1800s. Annie smiled as she ran her hand over the old school desk that stood in one corner.

"This looks just like one my friend used to have when she lived here." Looking closer, she saw that the letters EWB were carved into the top. "This is the same one. I'm sure of it. Susan and I used to try to figure out what the initials stood for."

Sandy perched on the edge of a ladder-back chair that looked to be of an age with the desk. "That's not surprising.

Most of this stuff was in the house when we bought it. I'd guess that the previous owners bought it furnished too."

"You're probably right. Susan wouldn't have needed a houseful of furniture."

"Not where she was going."

Annie turned to look at her. "Where she was going?"

"I—my husband said he's heard people talking in town, asking about your friend and saying she went off to marry a rich man. I guess she wouldn't have wanted stuff like this in some fancy family mansion."

"Probably not."

"It seems like it all should be here anyway." There was again something tentative in Sandy's smile. "It belongs with the house."

"Susan would be glad to know things are still the same as when she lived here."

"Is that what you came to talk to me about?"

"No. Not really. I mean, I appreciate your letting me come in for a minute. It brings back some really happy memories from when Susan and I played here."

"I'm glad."

Annie returned her smile, but Sandy quickly looked away.

"I came because I'm a little bit worried about you."

"Why would you be worried?"

"When I was here before, you seemed concerned about something. I don't want to pry into your personal business, but I did want you to know that I'd like to be your friend."

Annie wished Sandy would turn around and face her, but she only stared into the fireplace and didn't say anything.

"I guess I've been thinking about Susan a lot lately,

since I've been trying to find her," Annie added. "I used to come up to visit my grandmother in Stony Point when I was growing up. I was kind of an outsider here, just coming in the summers and all. My grandmother got me to invite Susan to play with me and my other friends. Gram tried to include her as much as possible while she was in Stony Point, and I think she'd feel the same way about you if she were still here."

"Your grandmother's dead now?"

Annie nodded. "I came here to settle her estate and fix up the house. I might sell it. I haven't decided yet."

"I'm sorry she's gone. She must have been nice."

"She was. And she cared about people. You know what?"

Annie waited until Sandy finally faced her again; then she smiled.

"If she were here, I bet Gram would invite you over for some coffee and a piece of pie and show you how to cross-stitch or something."

Sandy's face turned pink, but she seemed shyly pleased. "You think so?"

"I'm sure of it. It's what I'd like to do, if you'll come."

The warmth in Sandy's face turned to wariness. "That's nice of you, but I don't think—"

"I mean, I guess I'd have to teach you to crochet or knit because cross-stitching isn't my specialty, but if you like it better, Alice could show you."

"Really, I just don't—"

"Everybody should have a friend." Annie's throat tightened. "I lost track of Susan when she needed one most."

Sandy ducked her head, and Annie couldn't help

staring. What was it about the gesture that tickled Annie's memories?

"You know, sometimes you remind me of her—of Susan."

"Why would you think that?"

"Maybe it's because she's been on my mind so much lately. Maybe because you're out here alone in her old house."

"Maybe." Sandy looked her straight in the eye for perhaps the first time. "Maybe it's because there's a little bit of a family resemblance."

"Family resemblance?"

Annie stared at Sandy, studying her face. Maybe that was it. She had Susan's fine features and dark blue eyes. Except for Sandy's dark hair, Susan might look a lot like this now if she had lived.

"Susan always told me that, besides her aunt and her parents, she didn't have any family."

"It's not something her father or mine liked to talk about. Dad and I never talked about it even when I was older." Sandy shrugged. "I only saw Susan a couple of times anyway."

"Your father and her father were—" Annie raised one eyebrow.

"Brothers. But they didn't know anything about each other until their father died. Their father, my grandfather, was Sterling Morris. He was married to Mary."

"Grammy Mare. I remember Susan telling me about her. She passed away the summer Susan and I met."

Sandy glanced at Annie, and then the words came out in a rush. "Five years after he married Mary, he also married Laura. And, no, he and Mary never divorced. He was a truck driver, so it was fairly easy for him to spend time with both of his families and not have to explain the times he was away from home. Either home."

Annie fought to keep the astonishment off her face. She didn't want to make Sandy regret her decision to open up about herself and her family.

"Wow." Annie gave her a small, reassuring smile. "I guess you'll find a skeleton or two in every family closet if you go back far enough."

"My dad, Sterling's son Jim, found out about the first family when his father died. Evidently Mary didn't care to have him and Laura show up at the funeral. Things got ugly, and Dad just walked away. After my Grandma Laura died, Dad's brother Jack tried a couple of times to get in touch with him, I think, but Dad didn't see the point. Jack had the house and the legal name and everything else. All Dad got was the embarrassment of the situation."

"Is that how you ended up living here?"

"Why shouldn't I?" There was a flash of defiance in Sandy's usually mild eyes. "My ancestors built this place. My family is buried out back there. No matter what my grandfather did, I'm a Morris as much as any of them. As much as Susan was."

Annie put one hand on Sandy's shoulder. "I think she'd like it, knowing that you're here."

Sandy smiled faintly and let out a slow breath. "I hope so. I love this house and that it's been in our family for so long. It means a lot to me, too, to keep up those graves back there. They shouldn't belong to strangers. They're my people."

"Of course they are."

"But, um, I'd really rather you not say anything about what I told you, especially to the folks in town. It's been a while back now, but I don't want anyone to think any less of the Morrises because of what my grandfather did."

"You don't have to worry. I understand. And I'm glad you felt you could tell me about them."

"I always thought—" Sandy dropped her eyes. "I mean, you seem like you've always been easy to talk to."

"So does that mean you'll accept my invitation?" Annie grinned. "I have a pie recipe that's to die for."

"I appreciate it, but really … I really prefer to stay at home."

"But—"

"And I need to start getting dinner ready. Tom will be back before long."

It was only the middle of the afternoon, but Annie took the hint and stood up. She was pleased, after all, that Sandy had felt she could share some of her family history. No need to overwhelm the woman in their first real conversation. Still, there was one thing she couldn't help asking about.

"You said you had met Susan a couple of times. When was that?"

"When?" Sandy's forehead wrinkled. "I don't remember exactly. Once when I was in grade school. Once when I was grown up, nineteen or twenty or something. Why?"

"Was it here in Stony Point? That last time?"

Sandy nodded.

"Did you talk to her much?"

"Not really. I just came with Dad. His brother had invited him."

"Did she seem … upset to you?"

"Upset? No. She was quiet but polite. She just seemed normal to me. Why?"

"I don't know. It's probably nothing."

"What?"

Annie hesitated, but surely Sandy knew what had happened to Susan.

"You know Susan drowned, right?"

Sandy nodded, blank faced.

"It was right after her parents and her Aunt Kim died," Annie said. "In August of 1989."

There was a slight flicker of emotion in Sandy's eyes, but again she answered only with a nod.

"That had to be a pretty hard time for her," Annie added, still watching her face.

"It would be for anyone, wouldn't it? But I couldn't tell you about her then. The last time I saw her, her parents were still alive."

"And her aunt?"

Again Sandy shrugged. "I don't know if she was alive then or not. They didn't mention her, and she wasn't living here."

"No, she was in New York. Susan lived with her while she went to school there."

"OK," Sandy nodded. "So what does this have to do with what you wanted to ask me?"

Annie took a deep breath. She'd just have to say it and get it over with.

"With all that happening to her, I'm just wondering if

there's any chance she might have taken her own life."

"Susan?" Sandy considered for a minute. "No. No, I don't think she'd do something like that. I mean, I guess just about anybody might think about it when they're in hard times." She shrugged. "Sometimes just making the pain stop can seem worth it."

"But you said you didn't really know her?"

"That's true, but she was a Morris. She wouldn't have killed herself. She would have figured out how to deal with whatever was going on in her life, no matter what it was."

Annie squeezed Sandy's arm. "I hope you're right. I just … I feel bad that Susan and I drifted apart the way we did. I wish I had been there for her through everything. I feel like we could have been friends all our lives. Did I ever tell you why I've been looking for her?"

Sandy shook her head.

"I found her letters up in my grandmother's attic. They reminded me of how much fun we had back when we were girls, and I wanted to know she was OK. I wanted to see if we could be friends again. She had been kind of lonely back then, and I wanted to make sure she wasn't still."

Sandy swallowed hard. "Do you always take in strays?"

Annie's eyes twinkled. "I come from a long line of stray-taker-inners."

For the first time since Annie had met her, Sandy laughed.

Annie zipped up her jacket and turned toward the front door. "Thanks for letting me come in. And truly, I don't ever want to impose on you or your privacy, but I'd like us to be friends. If you ever need anything or just want to talk, please let me know."

"You'd better go."

Sandy's face was emotionless once again. She had obviously had enough company for one day.

Annie hurried out onto the porch and down the steps to her car. Sandy stood in the front door watching her. Then, just as Annie drove away, she waved one hand.

"Thank you for the cookies."

~ 13 ~

Before she was halfway home, Annie's cell phone rang. She pulled over to the side of the road and answered it.

"Annie, it's Mary Beth. Is, um, everything going all right?"

"It's OK. I'm on my way home."

"Whew. Tom just left here, and I wanted to let you know."

"Wow, I was hoping I'd be home before he headed this way. I'd better take a side street and come around the back way. I don't want him seeing me coming down the road from his house."

"Good idea. Call me when you get home."

"Will do."

When Annie had first visited the old Morris house alone, she had seen an old white pickup parked behind the house. When she and Alice first arrived at the house, the truck hadn't been there, but she had seen it after Tom Maxwell had "encouraged" her and Alice to refrain from visiting in the future. Now she kept on the lookout for such a vehicle, but nothing even remotely resembling it crossed her path.

She was almost giddy when she reached Grey Gables.

"You sound like you've been running," Mary Beth said as soon as she answered the phone. "Are you OK?"

Annie laughed. "I guess I'm a little breathless. It takes a

lot of energy to sneak around, you know?"

Mary Beth chuckled. "How'd it go?"

"Pretty well, I think. Sandy talked to me and actually let me come into the house."

"Really? You're making progress."

"It's interesting, too, that she has a lot of the same furniture Susan's family used to have. I guess it's been in the house since it was built. It was pretty amazing to see it looking just about the way I remembered it."

"You don't think there's anything weird going on, do you?"

"I'm still not sure. But the only way I know to find out is to get Sandy to trust me, to be a friend to her, and to listen. I just want to let her know that I want to help, that we *all* want to help, any way we can."

"Sounds like what Betsy would have done."

"Gram was the best at making people feel at home. I hope I've learned at least some of that from her. One thing I learned is that it takes a while. I may have to make a few more visits. How are things going with the cabinets? Do I have a little more time?"

"Another workday at least. I think, anyway. But Tom said he won't be able to come back until next week sometime."

"How did it go? Was he … OK?"

"He doesn't talk much, that's for sure. But he's polite and businesslike, and from what I can see, he does a good job."

"Hang on, Mary Beth. Somebody's at the door."

It was Roy Hamilton.

"I hope you don't mind me dropping by, Annie. The chief wanted me to tell you what he found out about that drowning in South Carolina."

"Thanks for coming by. Come in." Annie put her phone to her ear. "Mary Beth? Can I call you back in just a second?"

"Sure thing. I wouldn't want to interfere in a budding romance."

"You're *so* hilarious," Annie deadpanned. "Anyway, I'll call you right back. Thanks."

She hung up the phone and smiled at Roy.

"Come sit down. What did you find out?"

"Not a whole lot, I'm afraid." He followed her into the living room and sat next to her on the sofa. "The report pretty much echoes what was in that newspaper article. She drowned while her boyfriend was asleep below deck. There was a little bit of a squall around midnight, a pretty stiff wind, and over she goes. Not much to it."

"Did they mention any possibility that it was suicide?"

"No. The report says they asked the boyfriend about it. He said there was no note, nothing about her behavior that would indicate she wanted to kill herself. She never said she didn't want to live, never talked about wanting to end it all. Do you think she would have?"

"I don't know. I've talked to Reverend Wallace. To people who knew her, and there's no indication that she might have. But she seemed to have changed too, around the time her parents died. She seemed more withdrawn, less like herself. She canceled her wedding plans without warning."

"Grief strikes different people different ways. If you don't have more to go on than that, I wouldn't think it was very likely she killed herself. Sure, it's possible, but I don't see any indication of it, and I've dealt with all kinds since

I've been in this line of work." He put his hand over hers. "Look, for whatever reason, the bottom line is that she's dead. Not just gone, but long gone. Why does it matter whether or not she killed herself?"

She moved her hand away from his and stood up. "How about some coffee? I know I need some."

"That'd be great. Thanks."

She took her time filling the cups, replenishing the sugar bowl and the little stoneware cream pitcher Gram had always used, and then putting everything on a tray. Why did it matter how Susan had died? Why did it matter *why* Susan had died? Why couldn't she move on? She carried the tray back into the living room and set it down on the table in front of Roy.

"Ah, thank you." He picked up a cup and took a sip. "That's good."

"Thank you."

She drank from her own cup, not saying anything for a long moment.

"You know, Roy, it's a good question, and to be honest, I don't know why it matters. Maybe it just bothers me to see someone so completely disappear without knowing more about what happened to her." She let a little bit of a smile turn up her mouth. "My grandmother used to own this house. She always told me I was more stubborn than a snapping turtle when I wanted to know something. I guess that hasn't changed after all these years."

"Your grandma's place, huh?" He looked around the room, nodding in approval. "Must be nice to have a family home, something that's been around a long time. I've always moved a lot, but at my age you get a little tired of that. Stony Point seems like a good place to settle down."

"You're not from this area?"

"Nah. I was born in Tucson, and I've lived all over. Never did find the right place, or the right person." He glanced at her. "Till now."

"Stony Point's a good town. Lots of good people too. Can't argue with the choice, even though I may not be staying long."

"No?"

"Once I get the house fixed up and cleaned out, I'll probably head back to Texas."

"But what about your friend? You still haven't really found out everything you want to know."

She shrugged. "Maybe, as you say, there's just not anything more to know."

"There's those notes you got."

"Yes. And that does bother me."

"See? If you're a snapping turtle like your grandma said, you'll have to find out who left those for you before you can leave."

"Have you ever had a case with anonymous notes like those?"

"A time or two. Most of the time it's pretty obvious who'd send something like that."

"But not now."

"No," he admitted. "Not this time. Susan didn't have any family. The only one she left behind is that boyfriend of hers."

"Fiancé."

"Fiancé then. But he's about as far from here as you can be and still be in the continental U.S. Pretty unlikely that he'd be slipping by here to leave you little love notes."

"Then who could it be?"

"Who knew Susan when she lived here?"

"Not that many people, as far as I can find out. And after she came back from school in New York City, she wasn't here long. And she drowned way down in South Carolina. If there was something suspicious about her death, what would someone here have had to do with it?"

Roy drained his cup and returned it to the tray. "You have to consider the cranks out there, too, you know. Peggy's been talking up this whole thing about Susan Morris for a while now. Maybe somebody in town just doesn't like the idea of a busybody, if you'll pardon the expression, digging up the past. Especially if that busybody is an outsider."

"True enough. I guess you've gotten a little of that 'outsider' treatment yourself since you've been here, haven't you?"

He grinned. "Not so much I can't handle it. I figure once people get to know me, they can't help being smitten."

She finished her own coffee and got up. Whether or not he meant that to apply specifically to her, now seemed like a good time to break off the conversation.

"Thanks for telling me what you found out, Roy." She put both of their cups on the tray and picked it up. "If you guys find out anything else about Susan, please let me know."

She smiled firmly, and he stood too.

"Thanks for the coffee, Annie. If we get any break-throughs on the notes, I'll buzz you." He gave her one of his ever-present grins. "And if you feel like company, you know where to find me."

She smiled and waved as he drove away. Peggy had been right from the start about his not being able to take a hint. Annie didn't want to hurt his feelings, but he was certainly single-minded when he wanted to be. She'd have to keep her distance for a while.

*   *   *   *

The next meeting of the Hook and Needle Club renewed Annie's resolve to distance herself from Officer Hamilton. She had just taken her seat and started on her woefully neglected crochet when Gwen and Peggy converged on her.

"So?"

Gwen's blue eyes sparkled in anticipation, but Peggy frowned.

"I told her it's ridiculous, Annie, but she won't believe me."

Annie looked from one to the other. "Believe what?"

"You know." Gwen smirked. "You can't keep these things secret forever."

Annie stopped her work, placing her sweater-to-be in a multi-colored heap in her lap. "What are you two talking about?"

"I told her you and Roy don't have a romance going on."

"Peggy!"

Peggy shrugged. "She won't listen."

Annie turned to Gwen. "Listen."

"I don't mean I think you're getting married tomorrow

or anything. But it just seems to me, from what I've heard and with Roy talking about you all the time, there just might be a little something ..." Gwen raised her eyebrows.

Annie glanced at Alice, who held both hands up. "It didn't come from me. I wouldn't wish him on anybody."

Annie pressed her lips together. She couldn't tell them about the notes she had gotten. "Look, Gwen, whatever you've heard and whoever you've heard it from is wrong. I'm still trying to find out about Susan Morris. Chief Edwards' office is helping me. That's all there is between Roy and me. That's all, got it?"

Gwen looked down at the thick sock she was knitting. "Got it. Though I don't know why it would be such a bad thing. He seems like a nice guy."

"Well, he's all yours, if you don't think your husband will mind."

Gwen chuckled, and Annie's expression softened.

"Roy's all right, Gwen, but I'm just not interested in him."

"Yeah, OK. So, you're still trying to find out something about Susan?"

"Trying. I guess everybody knows by now that Susan drowned over twenty years ago." Annie glanced at Peggy, who ducked her head and concentrated on her appliqué. "I was hoping Stella would tell me more about Susan's fiancé today, since she knew his family. Where is she, anyway?"

"She and Edie Borman had to go meet with somebody in Portland about donations to the Cultural Center," Mary Beth said, "but she'll be at the meeting next week, I'm sure."

"That's OK. I can talk to her at the banquet. Did you decide what you're going to bring?"

With that, the talk turned to the coming festivities, and to Annie's relief, away from Roy Hamilton. She was glad the meeting wound up without anyone mentioning him again, but he was still on her mind when she walked across Main Street to the hardware store where she'd parked her car.

He was talking about her all the time now? Enough to make people think there was something between them? She'd definitely have to do something to dispel that notion. Piqued, she flung open her car door and leaned down to toss her purse and tote into the passenger seat.

When she straightened, she found herself face-to-face with Tom Maxwell.

— 14 —

Annie was speechless for a moment and then managed an uncertain smile. "Hello, Mr. Maxwell. Excuse me, I didn't see you there."

He narrowed his dark eyes at her. "You don't pay attention real good, do you?"

"I'm sorry?"

"I said, if you'd pay a little better attention, you'd save yourself a lot of trouble."

She glanced around. There were a few people on the street, not close, but within shouting distance.

She swallowed hard. "I don't know what you mean."

"I mean—" He glanced around, too, and then lowered his voice. "I mean that I would prefer that you leave my wife alone. She doesn't like company, and she doesn't want you coming around bothering her all the time. Is that clear enough, or do I need to write it all out for you?"

Feeling her heart pounding in her throat, Annie shook her head.

"I tried being polite before, Mrs. Dawson, but it didn't seem to work. So now I'm telling you straight out. Stay away from my wife."

Without waiting for a reply, he turned and stalked into the hardware store.

Annie stood frozen for a moment more; then she

scrambled into her car and locked herself in. Her pulse was racing, but she didn't want to sit around waiting for it to slow down and have him find her still there when he came out of the store.

She pulled out into the street, briefly considered stopping at Chief Edwards' office or at least Ian's, but decided to head straight home instead. By the time she pulled up in front of Grey Gables, her fear had galvanized into indignation, indignation that wasn't smoothed over when she found Roy Hamilton on her front porch.

"Roy?"

He came up to her car and opened the door for her. "You're home early."

She pressed her lips together, praying for a quick infusion of patience, kindness, gentleness, and self-control. Roy Hamilton was the last thing she needed on a day like this.

"What are you doing here?"

"I've been keeping an eye on your place. I thought maybe our guy might show up once you were gone, and I think he might have."

"Might have?"

"I really didn't see much. I'm pretty sure there was somebody on your porch just a minute ago. I drove around the block, trying to see if I could spot him, but he was gone."

"Who was it?"

"I don't know. He had on a dark jacket with the collar turned up and one of those stocking caps pulled down to his eyebrows. To be honest, I couldn't swear it was a man, but I'm reasonably sure it was."

"Was he tall or short?"

"I'd say average. About 5 feet 10."

"Heavyset?"

"No. Medium build. I guess it could have been something harmless. Maybe the guy was chasing his dog or something." He gave her a sheepish grin. "Maybe I'm too suspicious all the time."

"I hate to think I have to worry about my neighbors in a place like Stony Point." Annie sighed. "Maybe you're right, and it was a false alarm. I do appreciate you watching out for me though."

"It's my pleasure."

"Thanks. See you around."

"It's kinda cold out today, isn't it?" He rubbed his hands together. "Guess I'll head on home and make me some coffee."

"That's a good idea. I think I'll do the same thing."

She started to unlock the door and realized that he was still standing there. He looked a little forlorn, as if he wished his valor had earned him more than mere thanks. Again she smiled.

"Would you like to join me?"

He didn't have to be asked twice.

"You make a good cup of coffee, Annie. Sometimes a guy gets tired of those freeze-dried instant crystals."

She opened the door and stopped where she was. Someone had pushed another blank envelope through her mail slot.

"Don't touch it," he warned. He pulled his gloves out of his jacket pockets and put them on. Then he picked up the envelope. "Mind if I look inside?"

"Go ahead."

He flipped open the unsealed flap and pulled out the paper.

LET THE DEAD REST IN PEACE

Annie exhaled, her breath coming out in unsteady little puffs. Roy glanced at her.

"I guess it's referring to this Susan again. Is that the impression you get?"

"Yes. It's a little, um, unsettling. I don't know what to think."

"There's no real threat here," he reminded her. "Just like the last one. At least nothing that could be considered more than friendly advice."

"No. That's just it. I don't know whether to be scared or not. I guess I'd better talk to Chief Edwards about it."

"I'll let him know. In the meantime, I don't want you to worry about it. I'll check this for prints and see what else I can find out." He leaned toward her. "And I'll look after you."

She smiled, genuinely grateful. After her little chat with Tom Maxwell, it would be nice to know someone was watching out for her.

"Thanks, Roy. It's a little scary when you're on your own."

"You always have Boots, right?"

She managed a laugh. "She can be pretty tough when she needs to be, that's for sure."

Both of them studied the note again. The words were made up of letters cut from the newspaper. The paper they were pasted to was like any you'd find in almost every household in the country—plain white, no watermark. The envelope was equally nondescript, though this one was a safety envelope, like the second one she had received.

"Just like the ones you got before," he said. "That's the trouble with the cold weather."

"The cold weather? What do you mean?"

He wiggled his fingers at her. "Almost everybody is wearing gloves, so nobody leaves fingerprints."

She sighed. "Now what?"

"This isn't much to go on. Has anybody been telling you not to snoop around?"

"My daughter tells me that all the time, but she's in Texas right now, and I don't think she has anything to hide regarding Susan's death."

He chuckled. "Anyone else?"

"No more than usual. And only friends I know too well to suspect."

"Maybe they're friends who think you need a friendly warning. It's not all that threatening, you know."

"I hope it's not. It's a little vague, like the other one."

"You got a sandwich bag or something I can put this in?" He turned the note over and then back to the front. "A big one would be nice, so I don't have to fold it up more than it was."

She went into the kitchen and got him what he asked for, and he tucked the note inside.

"I'll dust this one for prints, too, but I can guarantee you there won't be any."

"Maybe we'll get lucky with this one."

"We'll see. Anyway, if you think everything's secure here, I'll head on over to the office."

"Thanks, Roy. Let me know what you find out."

She went to the door, holding it for him, and he handed her his card.

"That's got my home and cell numbers on it. I want you to know you can come to me if you need anything—anything at all. Or if you're just afraid to be home alone or something. I don't mind keeping an eye on you, if you'd like."

"That's sweet, Roy. It really is. But I'm all right. It's nice to know you're just down the street though."

So much for deflecting rumors.

He grinned as always. " 'To protect and to serve,' right?"

"Thanks."

"Oh, and remember to not say anything about this to anybody. We always like to keep something back that nobody knows about so we can make sure we've got the right guy if we catch him."

"All right. I won't say anything."

"Not even to Alice."

"But, Alice—"

"No, not to anybody. I mean it. If it gets out, it might scare the guy off. Or worse, it might make him do something stupid. So far, this has been pretty mild stuff. No threats. Nothing specific. We don't want to push him into something worse."

Annie nodded. "I'll keep it quiet. You just let Chief Edwards know about it."

"I'll take care of everything. Don't worry."

He went whistling out to his car, and soon she was alone in the house. More than ever, she wished Wayne were with her.

*   *   *   *

Let the dead rest in peace.

Why couldn't she do just that? But it still didn't make sense. Susan was gone. She had no family left except Sandy Maxwell, and nobody in town knew about that relationship. Was there something about the family that maybe Sandy didn't want anyone to know?

That couldn't be it. If Sandy hadn't told her about it, Annie wouldn't know there was a family connection in the first place. Besides, she wasn't looking into their family history, just Susan's death, and there was nothing to tie Sandy to that.

Annie rubbed her eyes. She needed to just drop the issue and get back to her regularly scheduled life. Susan was gone. It didn't matter.

Let the dead rest in peace.

Maybe she wouldn't drop the issue. Not quite yet anyway. There was still the anonymous prankster, or worse, to be found. Chief Edwards said he would be looking into the matter, but he hadn't been too encouraging. Resources in a little place like Stony Point were probably stretched too thin already to make a minor nuisance a priority, and it was likely that Roy was spending way too much time on it as it was.

But obviously, someone did care about Annie's investigation. She had to know why. If there was some indication that Susan's death was more than just an accident, maybe it would give her a clue about who might want something like that kept secret.

Before she lost her nerve, she dug out Archer Prescott's

cell phone number and dialed it. It took him four rings to answer.

"Mr. Prescott? This is Annie Dawson."

"Annie. How are you?"

"I'm fine. I'm sorry to bother you, but—"

"Now what did I tell you? I said you were welcome to call me anytime."

"Well, yes, Mr. Prescott, but—"

"And I told you to call me Arch, right?"

"Yes."

He was just being nice, she was sure, but he was obviously used to people obeying him most of the time.

"Now, Annie, what can I do for you? Have you found out anything new about Susan?"

"I hate to ask you this. I don't want to open up old wounds more than I have already, but I was wondering if you had ever considered the possibility that Susan may have taken her own life."

He was silent for a long moment.

"I remember the police asking me that at the time. I couldn't imagine it. She never said anything about wishing herself dead. She didn't leave any kind of note."

"But she had just lost her aunt and then both of her parents. Wouldn't that be a reason for her to be depressed?"

"No. Why should she be? Sad, certainly. That was to be expected, but clinically depressed? I don't think so, but I'm not an expert."

"I was talking to our Reverend Wallace about her the other day. Do you remember him? He remembers you."

"Wallace, huh? I'm not sure. I know I talked to the

reverend at the church in Stony Point about us getting married there. Could have been Wallace. Why? Does he have any reason to think Susan may have killed herself?"

"No. No, I don't think so, but he told me he thought she was different those last few weeks before you and she were to have been married. He said you had arranged for him to do your wedding, and then Susan called him and canceled the whole thing. Why do you think she did that?"

Prescott exhaled heavily. "I told you that already. It's no big mystery. She wanted a big wedding. That's why we were sailing down to Florida."

"The big wedding wasn't your idea?"

"You know how it is with us guys. All that fluffy stuff is for the woman. They usually want to be queen for a day with all the trimmings. I didn't much care either way, but I knew what it meant to Susan. After all she'd been through, I wanted to do something for her that would make her happy. I had thought getting married at her hometown church was what she wanted, so that's what I fixed up for her. Then, when I realized she wanted something with all the bells and whistles, I fixed that up for her. Do you really think she could have drowned herself on purpose?"

"I don't know. I was just wondering. She had no family left except a cousin she hardly knew."

"Cousin?"

Annie bit her lip. "Um—"

"What's this about a cousin? Susan didn't have any cousins."

"Well, actually, she did. I guess she never talked about this particular part of the family."

Since it was too late to put the cat back into the bag, Annie went ahead and told him about Sandy and Susan's grandfather and his two families.

"I had no idea. So what's this cousin's name?"

"Sandy. I don't guess Susan ever mentioned her to you."

"No. And you say she lives nearby now?"

"Out at Susan's old house on Elm Street. Do you remember it?"

"Oh yes, I remember the house. I remember it very well. I just don't remember any cousin Sandy."

"She and her husband moved here almost ten years ago."

"That's kind of a coincidence, isn't it?"

"Not really. Sandy tells me she wanted the house because of the family link. I guess with her connection to the Morrises being a little, um, unusual, family ties are important to her. And that unusualness was why I wasn't supposed to say anything to anybody. I hope you won't mention it to anyone."

"Out here?" He chuckled. "People wouldn't even blink at a family history like that, and I don't know who I'd tell it to in the first place. But I give you my word, nobody will hear about it from me. So what's this cousin like?"

"Pretty quiet. A real homebody, evidently. She works in her garden mostly. Her husband does handyman work in the area, and she keeps house. She didn't have all that much to say."

"Ah. A plump little housewife. That's nice."

"No, not plump. She's tall and slim. Actually, she favors Susan a little bit, from what I remember anyway. There's a definite family resemblance."

"And what does she say about Susan? Does she think she committed suicide?"

"No. She didn't know her very well. They only met a couple of times, but she says Susan was a Morris and would have figured out some way to deal with her problems rather than killing herself."

There was silence on the other end of the line. Then Prescott chuckled once more. "That does sound like Susan, as a matter of fact."

"It's too bad the two of them didn't have the chance to grow up together."

"Yes, too bad. Susan missed out on so much." He sighed. "There was so much I wanted her to have, so much we could have done if only things had been different. But things don't always work out the way we want them to, do they? Things happen. People … don't understand what's important in life, and that we can't let the petty things get in the way."

"I'm sure Susan knew how you felt about her. That's what's important."

"I wish she knew how important she is to me still."

"That's sweet." Annie hesitated, trying to think of something to say that would be comforting and not too saccharine, coming up with nothing. "Well, thank you for talking to me again. I hope I haven't brought back too many difficult memories for you."

"No, I can understand wanting to know the truth about what happened to someone you've lost track of. And don't worry about mentioning Susan's cousin to me. As far as I'm concerned, she never had one."

"Thanks, Mr. Prescott." She smiled to herself. "Arch."

"Goodbye, Annie."

Annie hung up the telephone. So was Susan's death an accident or not? She still knew nothing for certain either way, and there had to be some means of finding out. The question lurked in the back of her mind for the rest of the day. It was still there when she finally sat down that evening to work on her new sweater.

As usual, Boots wriggled up next to her in the over-stuffed chair in front of the living room fire. Annie stroked the gray-velvet head, eliciting some purring chatter.

"What do you think, Miss Boots? Am I wasting my time wondering about all this?"

Boots merely blinked her eyes and then laid her head on Annie's lap.

Careful to keep her yarn out of reach of curious paws, Annie began to crochet again. Who would want her to stop investigating Susan's death? Her thoughts turned again to Sandy Maxwell. Were there family secrets that Sandy didn't want getting out? Perhaps it was Mr. Maxwell who didn't appreciate the attention. And what was going on between him and Sandy?

Annie shook her head. He hadn't known Susan since he hadn't come to live in the house on Elm Street until ten years after her death. Who besides the Maxwells had any connection to Susan at all?

There was only Prescott. Annie hadn't even known he existed until after she had received the second note, and until she called him, he hadn't known about her. Besides, he sounded eager to know if Annie found out more about Susan and not as if he wanted to cover it all up.

After a while, Annie laid her sweater in her lap, leaned her head back, and closed her eyes. It was a puzzle, that was for certain.

She didn't realize she had dozed off until she heard Boots growl. The cat had been sound asleep, but now she was standing up with her head thrust forward, staring fixedly at the front door.

"What is it, baby?"

Boots didn't move, but she didn't growl anymore. Maybe she had just had a bad dream.

Annie scratched her behind the ears. "Go back to sleep, kitty."

She tried to push the cat back down into her lap, but Boots resisted, and the fur down her spine and along the length of her tail puffed out like gray eyelash yarn.

In spite of herself, Annie felt her heartbeat quicken. This was Stony Point, not New York City or Chicago. People here left their doors unlocked and weren't afraid to walk alone at night.

She reached to stroke the cat again. "Boots ..."

Once again, Boots growled.

Annie set her crochet on the end table beside her and put Boots down on the floor. She'd call Alice. Then when she took a look around outside, at least somebody would be watching out for her. No, she couldn't call Alice. It was after midnight. Unless it was a genuine emergency—and the cat's growling probably didn't qualify—it would be rude to disturb anyone, even a best friend, this late.

She picked up the phone anyway and dialed Alice's number, all but the last digit. Then she checked the front door. It was locked, but she slipped the dead bolt into place as well. She went out to the kitchen and checked the back door. She must have left that unlocked when she'd been out in the yard earlier in the day. She locked it, and then turned off the kitchen lights.

For a few seconds, she stood there in the dark just listening, but there wasn't a sound anywhere in the house. Outside, the wind was rustling the tree limbs, and the sliver of a moon did little to illuminate the yard. Maybe it was just her imagination after all. She put her hand on the light switch and then froze.

She had definitely heard something, and it was definitely inside the house. Just before she dialed the last digit of Alice's number, she saw a dark silhouette in the doorway to the kitchen.

It was a little four-footed silhouette with a ball of yarn in its mouth.

"Boots," she breathed, and she went over to pick up the cat. "You scared me to death. And that is *not* for you to play with."

She put the phone down on the kitchen table and carefully disengaged the yarn from the cat's mouth. Then she walked back into the living room and found that her crochet hook was underneath the coffee table. Well, that would account for the clattering noise she had heard.

"You, missy, had better learn to leave my stuff alone." She held up the hook for the cat to see. "This isn't a toy, and I don't need you to make me nervous."

Undaunted, Boots batted at it until Annie pulled it away from her.

"You are obviously not listening, so we're going to bed."

Holding Boots in one arm, she put the yarn and the hook into her crochet bag and closed it up, protecting it from curious little paws.

"OK, baby cat, nighty-night."

She turned out the lights in the living room and froze once more. She was sure she had seen something move outside the window. Was it just the bushes? Again she stood in the darkness, unmoving. Boots squirmed against her shoulder, but Annie wasn't quite ready to let her down. She wasn't quite ready to feel totally alone.

As swiftly as possible, she went back into the kitchen and picked up the phone she had left there. Once more, she dialed Alice's number and then hung up before it could ring.

No, she didn't know that someone was out there. The doors were locked. She hadn't actually seen anyone.

She trembled a little where she stood. Had those notes spooked her enough to make her imagine things that weren't there? Enough to make her feel unsafe in her own home?

But if someone was out there …

She went back through the darkened hallway and into the living room. Still holding Boots, she rummaged through her purse until she found the business card she had slipped into her makeup bag. Reading the number by the light from the hall, she dialed the phone. It rang only once.

"Hello?"

"Roy?"

"Well, Annie, what a surprise."

"I hope I'm not disturbing you, Roy. I know it's late and

everything, but I think there may be somebody in my yard, snooping around outside."

"Did you see anybody?"

"No. A little movement out there maybe, but I couldn't be sure it was actually a prowler. I didn't want to make an official call to the police if I wasn't sure."

"No, you don't want to do that. But if it would make you feel better, I'd be glad to come take a look around and make sure everything is secure. Maybe have a cup of coffee?"

As much as she didn't want to encourage him, she couldn't help the rush of gratitude at his offer. "Absolutely."

He showed up just a few minutes later. Annie didn't let Boots down until she went to open the door for him.

"Thanks for coming, Roy. I'm sorry to get you over here in the middle of the night."

"Not a problem. I was still up." He looked her over, obviously noting that she wasn't dressed for bed. "Looks like both of us are night owls."

"I guess I fell asleep in the chair. Boots woke me up growling at something."

"Does she usually do that?"

"No. Not unless there's something wrong. I never saw anything, though."

"You just get that coffee ready. I'll have a look around outside and be right back."

He was as good as his word. By the time the coffee brewed, he was sitting at the kitchen table eating goldfish crackers. She had offered him a choice of several things she had on hand, but he had specifically requested those. Little John and Joanna would find him a kindred spirit.

"I never saw a thing." He tossed a goldfish into the air and caught it in his mouth, making sure she had seen and properly appreciated his feat.

She acknowledged it with a distracted smile. "No footprints?"

"Only mine, I'm afraid. It could have been the wind. In all likelihood, it was just that, but I'm glad you called me. I'd rather be wrong on the side of caution than take the chance of you being over here alone if there was a problem."

"That's sweet of you, Roy. But I'm fine now. I've been pretty jittery ever since I started getting those notes, and now I don't know if I'm seeing things."

"Then again, something made your cat growl. They can be pretty inscrutable little things, I know, but they're pretty smart too. Sometimes they know things we don't."

"She is good at reading people." Annie frowned, looking around the room. "I'm a little surprised she's not here checking you out about now. She's usually really interested in visitors."

"Probably figured I wasn't worth bothering about."

"Everybody's worth bothering about."

He grinned appreciatively and pushed his nearly empty coffee cup toward her. "That's good stuff on a cold night."

"I'm glad you liked it." She stood up and picked up the cup, but she didn't offer him more. "Thanks again, Roy, for coming by. I'm sure I'll be fine now."

He looked a little disappointed, but he was polite enough to take the hint.

"Did you find out anything else about your friend?"

"No. That's what's so frustrating about all this. If

whoever is sending the notes knew how little I actually know about anything, he—or she—would quit. Why try to scare me if there's nothing to scare me away from?"

Roy shrugged and zipped his jacket up to his chin. "We might never find out why. Or who."

"In that case, I'm sorry to have wasted so much of your time."

"Don't you believe it." He gave her a wink. "Not a minute of it has been a waste."

"Thanks. I don't know why I'm so jumpy lately."

"Anybody would be, with what's been going on," he said as they walked back to the front of the house. "I'd be surprised if you weren't."

"I guess you learn a lot about people in doing police work."

"Oh yeah. You figure out what makes them tick. After a while, it gets to be pretty predictable."

When they reached the door, before she could do more than unlock it, he turned her toward him.

"Annie, I—"

Suddenly, he was leaning toward her, his lips almost touching hers as she pulled away. Before the shock really registered, he released her.

"Now you know."

She had an almost uncontrollable urge to laugh. Not because she thought it was funny, but because she didn't quite know what else to do. But she held it in. She didn't want to hurt him, even though she knew she would have to. There was no need to humiliate him on top of that.

"Roy."

That was all she said, but he could obviously read everything in her expression.

"Don't say anything. You don't have to say anything right now."

"I have to, Roy. I appreciate your help with everything that's going on, but I don't want you to imagine that there's any possibility of anything more than that. I told you about my husband, Wayne. There isn't room for anyone else in my heart right now. There may never be."

He ducked his head. "I understand how you feel. I just wanted you to understand how I feel."

"I may not even be here in Stony Point much longer. It would be silly for us to get involved, knowing that I might be 1,600 miles away next month."

"But you might not be."

"But that wouldn't change anything. I still wouldn't be ready for a new relationship."

She didn't want to have to say more, but she knew that, even if she was ready to fall in love again, it wouldn't be with him. She softened her expression. "Roy, it's sweet of you, but I don't want to lead you on. I don't want you to keep hoping—"

"I guess I can if I want to." There was a shadow of a grin once more on his face. "You'd get to like me if you gave me a chance. You know you would."

She smiled too. She did like him better than she had when she had first met him, but liking was all it would ever be. "You'd be better off finding somebody else, Roy. Somebody who's looking for a guy like you. Somebody who's going to be here a long time."

"You can't leave now, you know. We haven't solved your mystery yet."

"No, I suppose you're right about that. As long as I keep getting these notes, I know there's something somebody doesn't want me to find out. And that just makes me more determined to find out what's going on."

He leaned one elbow against the door frame. "That's part of what I like about you. You don't give up."

"Roy." She exhaled heavily and looked directly into his eyes so there would be no mistake. "Sometimes I have to give up. Sometimes what I want just isn't going to happen."

"But you don't give up at the first bump in the road either, or you'd never get anywhere. Look, I'm not asking you for anything. Let me do my job on this case. Let me keep an eye out for you while it's going on. Who knows where we'll be when it's all over?"

The two of them stared at each other, both refusing to flinch. Finally, Annie shook her head.

"You win. For now. But I'm telling you right up front, I just don't see us as anything but friends."

"But we *are* still friends, right? You're not mad at me?"

"No, I'm not mad. I just want you to understand how things are." OK, so she was a pushover. "And yes, we're still friends."

"Does that mean you'll let me take you to the banquet tomorrow night?"

"Roy." She closed her eyes and shook her head. The man was incorrigible. "What did we just talk about?"

"Well, you *are* going, aren't you?"

"Alone."

"All right. I guess I'll just have to see you while you're there." He opened the door. "Good night."

"Good night, Roy."

She locked and bolted the door once he was gone. After this thing with the notes and the prowlers, who may or may not be out there, was all over, she would have to have a nice long talk with Officer Hamilton. No matter how unpleasant a task it was, she was going to have to make sure he knew how utterly impossible his hopes were when it came to the two of them ever having any sort of romance.

She was not going to give him any room to say she had led him on. Or that she had taken advantage of his kindness. Or that she had indicated the slightest interest outside of general and not remotely close friendship. He hadn't been the least bit shy in expressing his feelings, and she had already told him straight out that she wasn't looking for a new relationship, but it hadn't seemed to dampen his ardor in any perceptible amount.

Annie saw Boots investigating her crochet bag and went to pick her up.

"At least he's being a gentleman about it, Boots, even if he doesn't seem to want to take never for an answer. He'd just better not have anything *special* in mind for the banquet tomorrow night."

Boots made a little complaining meow but didn't resist being taken upstairs to bed.

~ 15 ~

The community center was decked out in orange, red, and yellow streamers punctuated with bouquets of dried wildflowers tied with raffia. Hurricane lanterns and Alice's little cornucopias ornamented every table, and colorful squash and pumpkin groupings sat on top of bales of hay in the corners. A smiling scarecrow lounged on either side of the podium and a stuffed crow in a straw hat was perched on the microphone.

Annie smiled. She had helped set up the tables and the chairs around them earlier in the day. Then the decorating committee, led by Alice, had shooed everyone else out of the building to finish up.

It looked nice, even if it was a little kitschy—warm and casual and colorful and fun. Who could ask for more? And it smelled wonderful too. The aroma of turkey and ham, baked squash and peach cobbler along with myriad other home-cooked dishes made the large room a treat for the nose as well as for the eyes. Annie knew from experience that everything would taste as good as it smelled. Whether it was Texas or Maine or anywhere between, nobody cooked better than church ladies.

"What do you think?" Alice stood with her arms crossed looking over the banquet hall. "Too much hay?"

"It looks great. And of course, you have to have hay.

Nothing says 'harvest' like big bales of hay and scarecrows."

Alice laughed. "Oh, we've decided to auction off your pies for donations for the food pantry. Is that OK with you?"

"Sure. Whatever helps out most."

"And they won't actually be *your* pies, you understand. They'll be Betsy Holden's famous homemade pies."

Annie chuckled. "If that gets the bidding up, that's fine too. Anything I can do to help?"

"I think we're all ready. Just waiting for the guest of honor."

Annie found herself a seat at one of the tables, and soon Ian spotted her from across the room. She returned his wave, and he made his way over to her.

"You ladies did a fine job fixing things up, as usual."

"I can't take any credit, I'm afraid." Annie pulled out a chair for him. "I didn't have much to do with the beautification portion of the operation, just the basic manual labor."

"And pies, I hear."

She laughed. "I can't take credit for those, either. Those are Gram's recipes, and she's the one with the reputation for her cooking."

"So what are you up to when you're not baking pies? How are things going with your investigation?"

"I think I'm spooking myself more than anything else. I was half convinced that somebody was prowling around my house last night."

Concern flashed into Ian's eyes. "Did you call the police?"

"Just Roy. I never actually saw anyone out there, and he's right down the street."

"And I suppose he jumped at the chance to come see you."

"He was nice enough to come by." Annie looked up and then smiled tightly. "And here he is now."

"Annie!" Roy waved from across the room and made his way toward her. "Good to see you again."

"Hi, Roy. Ian and I were just talking about what happened last night."

"Mr. Mayor." He extended his hand to Ian, who shook it coolly.

"Officer Hamilton. I understand you didn't find any sign of a prowler at Annie's."

"Nope. But I'll keep an eye on her till we figure out what's going on." He winked at Annie. "Meanwhile, I can't complain about some of the best coffee *and* best company I've had since I've been in Stony Point."

"She is good company," Ian said, his voice carefully pleasant. "You haven't forgotten about our rain check, have you, Annie?"

Both men looked at her, and she could feel the heat rise in her face. "No, not at all. I'll let you know about that."

Roy's eyes narrowed just the slightest bit, but he kept a slight smile on his face. "Sounds like running the city isn't keeping you busy enough these days, Mr. Mayor."

"Can't complain, Officer. Can't complain. How about you? I don't suppose you've found out anything more about the anonymous letter writer?"

"Nothing yet, but I've got my eyes open."

Annie saw Alice and Mary Beth making a fresh batch of punch and seized the opportunity. "Sounds like you two have business to talk about, and I see I'm needed at the drinks table."

She waved airily, and over their protests, made her escape.

Alice grinned at her when she got to their table. "You know neither of them was particularly interested in talking to the other."

"Hush and give me that pineapple juice."

She punched holes in the top of the can and started emptying it into the big cut-glass bowl. Just as she finished with a fresh batch of punch, Stony Point's chief of police came up to the table.

"Good evening, Mrs. Dawson." He lifted his empty plastic cup. "Am I too early for a refill?"

"Just in time." She gave the well-iced mixture one last stir and then dipped out as much punch as the ladle would hold. "How's that?"

He took a deep drink. "Excellent, thank you. It's good to see you again. And good to know it's outside of work."

"Yes, I'm glad to forget about the whole note thing, at least for tonight. Even Ian and Roy were talking about it." Annie glanced over to where the two men had been standing, but now Ian was talking to elderly Mrs. Snyder, and Roy was nowhere to be seen. "Anyway, tonight is just food and fun. No notes."

"I'm sorry we never found out anything for you on that. At least you haven't gotten any more."

She shook her head. "Not since Tuesday anyway."

"You had one on Tuesday? Why didn't you let me know?"

"Didn't Roy tell you?"

"No, he didn't."

"Maybe he didn't think it was that important. It was

pretty much the same stuff as the other two."

"You've had three of these things now?"

Annie wrinkled her brow. "I thought Roy was keeping you informed all this time. Maybe since you put him in charge of the investigation, he wanted to wait to talk to you about it until he had more to go on."

Chief Edwards' eyes narrowed. "I think Officer Hamilton and I need to have a little discussion right about now."

Annie looked around the hall and finally spotted Roy on the far side of the room with his back to her. He was talking to Wally Carson. "You didn't put him in charge of the investigation, did you?"

"No. Is that what he told you? Since I didn't hear about any other notes, I figured the thing had played itself out. Like I said, the officer and I need to discuss the matter."

"Do you mind if I go with you? I have a few questions of my own for Officer Hamilton."

Wally and Roy erupted into laughter as Annie and the chief of police approached them.

"Hey there, Chief." Wally slapped Edwards on the back. "I tell you, I thought I had some good stories, but Roy beats me all hollow."

Annie smiled tightly. "Evidently you both enjoy tall tales."

"No harm in a good fish story, I always say." Roy's habitual smile was a little uncertain as he looked from Annie to his chief and back again. "As long as everybody's amused by it and everything."

Chief Edwards' eyes were fixed on Roy. His face was stony. "Will you excuse us a minute, Wally?"

"Um, sure. Whatever you say, Chief."

Wally scurried over to where his wife was setting out appetizers. Voice low, he said something to her, and both of them pretended not to look in Annie's direction.

"What's been going on with Mrs. Dawson's case, Roy?"

Roy was unable to look his boss in the eye. "Just what I told you, Chief. It's been kind of quiet lately."

"You mean, except for those two notes you didn't tell me about?"

Roy glanced at Annie. "I, um, I didn't say anything because I was hoping to have a breakthrough before now. I thought it would be better if I solved the thing and then let you hear about it. No use bothering you when there's really nothing much to report."

"Nothing to report? 'Nothing,' as in that man you saw on my front porch?" Annie glared at him. "Or was there anybody there at all?"

"Annie—"

"What's been going on here, Roy?"

"It's not what you think."

"And what do I think? That there wasn't anybody on my porch that day but you? That there wasn't anybody prowling around my house last night *but you*? That you were the one writing those notes all along? Why don't you want me to find out about Susan, Roy?"

"No, no. You've got to listen to me. It wasn't like that. I didn't start it."

They had kept their voices at a conversational level, but it was clear that the people around them knew that the three were engaging in more than small talk.

"Let's go over to the office and talk about this," Edwards said. "That's not a suggestion, Officer."

As they walked toward the exit, Alice pulled Annie aside. "What's going on?"

"Just getting something straightened out." Annie realized that her expression must be tense to say the least. She forced a bit of a smile. "It's all right. We'll be back in a few minutes."

The town hall was just across the street from the church and its community center, and soon Annie, Roy, and Edwards were in the chief's office. No one had said anything during the walk over, but as soon as he had shut the door behind them, Edwards demanded an explanation from his officer.

"I know it sounds pretty lame, but I didn't mean anything by it."

"Why don't you want me to find out about Susan?" Annie insisted.

"What?" Roy laughed faintly. "No. Susan? I don't know anything about her. She's dead. What do I care?"

"Then why did you write those notes? Why were you threatening me?"

"I would never threaten you. You must know that. I thought—" He glanced at his chief and ducked his head. "Annie, do I have to explain?"

Edwards crossed his arms over his broad chest. "I want to know what's been going on here, Hamilton. What do you have to do with these notes?"

"I don't know what I was thinking. I swear I've never done anything like this before. I just—" Roy swiped one hand over his face. "I thought if I kept writing those notes, Mrs. Dawson would keep coming to me about them, especially if she thought I was in charge of the case. Then I'd be able to talk to her, and she wouldn't just blow me off. And I thought that, if she spent a little time with me, she might get to like me after all."

"And when did this plan come to mind?"

"It was after she brought in that first one," Roy admitted. "You gave it to me to analyze, and I realized—"

"Wait a minute. *After* the first one? That one wasn't yours?"

"No. I did the last two, but not the first one. That one, I swear, I've been all over it and there's just nothing traceable about it. That's what gave me the idea."

Annie had to clench her jaws to keep from boiling over. "So we're no closer to knowing who left that one for me?"

"No, I guess not."

"And really, there wasn't anybody on my porch that day?"

"Shoot, Annie." Roy managed a pale imitation of his usual grin. "You caught me right after I put that note through your mail slot. What else could I say?"

"And last night?"

"I figured you'd call me if you thought somebody was out there, and then maybe we could talk, spend a little time …"

He shrugged weakly, and she pressed her lips together, keeping her rising anger in check.

"What part of Terroristic Threat don't you understand, Officer?" Edwards glared at Roy. "How about Abuse of Authority? Sound familiar?"

"I wasn't trying to terrorize anybody. Annie, you don't believe that, do you?"

She sighed. "I have to admit that I wondered most of the time whether I was being threatened or just advised. But, Roy, no matter how mild they might have been, you know how scary it is to think somebody is stalking you. How could you do that to me? How could you lie to me like that and make me think you were looking out for me when all you were doing was making a way for yourself?"

Roy said nothing. There was nothing he could say. Chief Edwards broke the silence. "You have every right to press charges, Mrs. Dawson. We have a pretty good case here."

"What'll happen if I do?"

"Whether or not he's convicted, and he most likely would be, that would pretty much end his career as a policeman. We'd have to fire him, and it's pretty likely he wouldn't get hired on anywhere else."

Annie glanced at Roy. "And if I don't?"

"If you don't, he will have the opportunity to tender his resignation, and that will be the end of it."

Annie pressed her lips together. "And have him do something like this in another town?"

"No!" Roy ducked his head. Then he lifted it again. "No. Annie, I'm sorry. I mean, I'm really sorry. I know what I did was wrong, and there's no excuse for it, but I won't do it again. I wasn't trying to hurt you or anybody. You know that."

She looked away. She did know that. And she knew how small towns could be for outsiders, especially for an outsider who took a false step. But a police officer was supposed to abide by the law no matter what, not take advantage of his position.

"What do you want to do, Mrs. Dawson?" Edwards pressed, and he glanced at Roy once again. "Of course, he'll be suspended until this matter is resolved."

Roy's eyes pleaded with her, and she was forced to look away from them.

"Can I think about it for a day or two?"

Roy grabbed her arm. "I swear I didn't mean to hurt anyone, Annie. Especially not you."

She coolly detached his hold on her. "I'll let you know, Chief Edwards."

She went back to the church alone, glad it was not a long walk. What in the world was Roy thinking? Did he think any woman would appreciate being deceived, no matter how flattering the reason? But that was really just an irritation. More troubling was the knowledge that she still had no idea who had sent the first anonymous message she had received. She looked around the dark street, and the idea that someone was watching her came back with intensity. She was glad for the welcoming lights of the church building.

Ian was standing in the doorway. Had he been waiting for her?

She hurried her stride. "What are you doing out here?"

"Being a little bit nosy, I guess." He held the door open to let her in. "Everything all right?"

"Yeah, I guess." She dredged up a smile. "I guess you're a better judge of people than I am."

He glanced toward the town hall. The light in Chief

Edwards' office was still burning.

"Anything I can do to help?"

She exhaled slowly. "No. I'm just disappointed."

"Did Edwards ever find out anything about the anonymous note you got? I mean, besides that there weren't any prints on it?"

She considered telling him about the other notes and about Roy, but she decided that was between Edwards and his officer. If the chief of police wanted to discuss his department's disciplinary matters with the mayor, that was his business.

"No, they still haven't found out anything on that note."

"And you haven't heard anything more from whoever sent it to you?"

"No," she answered truthfully. "I don't think I'm any closer to figuring out who that was than when I got it in the first place."

"I hope you're being careful. Sometimes you find out more than you really want to when you're digging up the past."

"What do you mean?" Annie studied his face. Was this friendly advice or something more?

"Just that there are some real weirdos out there. I wouldn't want anything to happen to you. Sometimes it's best to keep out of things."

Mind your own business.

She narrowed her eyes. "Are you trying to tell me something?"

"Only that I worry about you." He gave her a puzzled smile. "Is that a bad thing?"

"I'm a big girl, Ian. I can take care of myself just fine without your help."

She stalked back into the banquet room and left him standing there staring after her.

When she came in, Alice smiled at her from behind the punch bowl.

"Where've you been? And where'd the police force go?"

"I think I'd better have some of that punch." Annie picked up the cup Alice had just filled. "I need to cool off."

"What's going on?"

"Do I look feeble?"

Alice snickered. "What?"

"Helpless?"

"Annie—"

"Incompetent?"

"What are you talking about? I'd say you've had too much punch already, except the only thing in it is pineapple juice, sherbet, and ginger ale."

"And where have you been, Annie?" Stella came up to the table with a covered casserole dish in both hands. "You missed Reverend Wallace's presentation."

"Oh, I'm sorry I did. Was he surprised?"

"He pretended well at least."

Alice chuckled. "It's nearly impossible to keep a secret around here."

"I had to take care of some business with Chief Edwards," Annie explained.

Stella lifted one silver eyebrow as she set the dish on the table. "About this Susan Morris still?"

"Sort of. It was another dead end." Better to leave Roy

and his adolescent antics out of the conversation for now. "I just wish I knew more about what she was feeling, what she was going through, right before she died."

"Whatever it was," Stella said, "she's at peace now, isn't she?"

"Yeah, well, I only wish I could be." Annie sighed. "I just know there's something more here than I've found out so far. But even talking to her fiancé hasn't really gotten me anywhere."

Stella pursed her lips and almost imperceptibly turned up her nose. "Archer Prescott."

"He seems like a nice guy."

"Self-absorbed, if you ask me."

Annie bit her tongue. She wasn't in the mood for Stella's prickliness tonight.

"Why do you say that?" Alice asked.

"Because he is."

"Maybe he's changed since you saw him last. How long has it been?" Annie managed a bit of a smile. "Maybe he's grown up a little after this long."

Stella didn't look convinced. "I don't know why he's got that whole company by himself, anyway. I always thought his brothers knew more about the business than he did, but I guess Jason thought otherwise."

"Jason?"

"Jason Prescott was a friend of mine and my husband's. He and his three boys—Archer, Scott, and Donny—ran the company until he died. But he left the business to Archer. Something about Scott and Donny needing to make it on their own, I think. You never could tell with Jason."

"Well, Archer Prescott seems to have done well." Annie set out a few clean cups. "These days, just about everybody owns something made by JFP."

"Yes, it's grown some since it was just a regional company. I guess a lot of men throw themselves into their work after a tragedy. But I heard he's married now. I don't know anything about her, but they have two or three children, I believe."

"Yes, he mentioned he had a wife," Annie said. "I'm glad."

"He has his brothers, too, but I don't think they're close. Not after their father passed on." Stella smiled fondly. "I always liked Scott and Donny. They were such polite boys."

Alice glanced at Annie. "What about Archer?"

"He's been very polite when I've talked to him," Annie said.

"Too polite, if you ask me." Stella shook her head. "I always told my husband he was just too polite. There's something sneaky about people who are too polite."

Annie couldn't help laughing. Leave it to Stella to remember something like that after more than twenty years.

Their conversation was interrupted by a tap on the microphone. Reverend Wallace smiled from behind the podium.

"If I may have your attention once more, I'd like to ask God's blessing on this delicious-smelling food before it gets cold."

There was a brief bit of shuffling as heads were bowed and eyes were closed, and then there was quiet. Reverend Wallace's rich voice rolled over the room, speaking words of thanksgiving and blessing and love that were balm to Annie's roiling emotions. When the amen was spoken and echoed by those around her, Annie lifted her head and caught Ian, at the next table, looking her way.

He quickly averted his eyes, but she could see the uncertainty in them. Hurt, too, if she was honest. He hadn't deserved being snapped at.

Annie went over to him. "I'm sorry, Ian. I was pretty short with you a few minutes ago."

"I didn't mean to say anything to upset you. Forgive me?"

She shook her head. "No, forgive me. It's been, uh … an interesting evening. But, no, you haven't done anything wrong. I've just let all this business with Susan and everything else get to me more than it should. That's no excuse to take it out on you."

"I think you'll feel a lot better with some of this great food in you. I know I will." He stood up, offering her his arm and a warm smile along with his forgiveness.

"Um, Ian—I really need to make a quick call. Will you wait for me just a minute? I promise I won't be long."

He looked puzzled but agreeable. "I'll be right here when you're ready."

She hurried into the deserted hallway and punched a telephone number into her cell phone.

"Stony Point Police."

"Chief Edwards? This is Annie Dawson. I've decided I don't want to press charges. If you'll just take care of things with Roy, I'd appreciate it very much."

"OK, Mrs. Dawson, if you're sure. You have every right—"

"I have every right to remember I need a little grace myself sometimes. I don't see any reason to drag all this out any longer, do you?"

"No, ma'am. I'll take it from here."

Annie exhaled, feeling the tension inside her suddenly dissipate. "Thank you. Thank you very much."

She hung up the phone, put it back into her purse, and then returned to the banquet room. Ian smiled as she approached him. She took his arm, and they got in line to be served.

~ 16 ~

Annie picked up the letters that lay on the floor in the entryway. As she did every morning these days, she made sure there weren't any unaddressed envelopes in the stack. Since Roy's confession at last night's banquet, only the first note was unaccounted for, and that one still troubled her.

Who had sent it? Why had he—or she—stopped after the first one? And what connection did this person have with Susan?

As she went through her daily chores, Annie asked herself those questions again and again. Again and again she kept coming back to Sandy Maxwell. She was Susan's cousin. She was the only tie to Susan in Stony Point. There had to be something she knew, something she wasn't saying, about Susan.

Where had Sandy been living at the time of Susan's death? She had never said anything about that, or about how she had found out that Susan had drowned. Had she searched for Susan as Annie had done? If so, what else did she know?

Annie put away the vacuum cleaner and picked up the telephone.

"A Stitch in Time. This is Mary Beth. How can I help you?"

"Hi, Mary Beth. It's Annie."

"Oh!" Mary Beth's voice dropped conspiratorially. "He's here. I was about to call you."

"Tom Maxwell?"

"His other job canceled on him, so he came by to finish up the cabinets today."

"That's perfect. I really need to talk to Sandy for a little while, and I don't want him finding me there again. Not after what happened on Tuesday."

"What happened on Tuesday?"

Annie laughed unsteadily. "After the meeting was over, I ran into him outside the hardware store. He told me straight out to stay away."

"Or what?"

"He didn't exactly say what he'd do, but judging by his tone of voice and the look in his eyes, it wouldn't be pretty."

"Did you tell the police?"

"No."

"Annie!"

"He has every right in the world to ask me to stay off his property, doesn't he?"

"Then maybe you should do just that."

"It'll be OK. As long as he's at your shop, I can talk to Sandy for a few minutes. I just need to ask her a few more questions; then I won't go back."

Mary Beth exhaled heavily. "Do you have your phone with you? It is charged up?"

"I'm good to go. You just make sure to give me a call if he leaves there."

"Will do. Be careful."

Annie hung up the phone and got herself cleaned up. After she had checked her cell phone one last time, she drove over to Sandy Maxwell's.

It was a beautiful day out, even if it was on the colder side of crisp. Hoping Sandy would be out in her garden, Annie didn't go up to the front door. Instead, she walked past the old oak where the swing had been and around the side of the house.

Sandy was spreading pine needles over one of her immaculate flower beds, mulching them before the real winter weather set in. She looked up when she heard the crunch of Annie's steps in the brown grass.

"Annie." She leaned her rake against the wall. "What are you doing here?"

"I'm sorry to drop in on you again, Sandy, but I need to talk to you."

Sandy dusted off her hands and gestured to the wrought-iron chairs on the back porch. "I don't know what there is to talk about. I didn't really know Susan, and I can't tell you anything about her."

She sat down and so did Annie.

"Is there any reason why you wouldn't want me to find out about her?"

Annie studied her face, awaiting her answer. Susan would probably look like her now if she were still alive. It was hard to tell. Those teen years were so long ago. But there was something about her that made Annie remember. It was more a feeling than anything tangible.

"Why would you think that?"

Sandy didn't answer right away, and when she did, her

voice contained a little thread of uncertainty.

"I don't know."

Somehow Annie couldn't see Sandy doing anything that would harm or threaten anyone. There was something gentle and easily hurt about her. She had seen the same thing in Susan all those years ago.

"I didn't tell you before, but someone left an anonymous note at my house a while ago. It was made up of letters cut from a newspaper pasted on a piece of blank paper. It said, 'Forget about Susan and mind your own business.' Who would have left me something like that?"

Sandy shook her head. "It wasn't me. I don't even drive."

"I'm not accusing you of anything. But I don't know anyone else with a connection to Susan here in Stony Point. You don't think your husband would have left something like that, do you?"

"No, of course not. Why would he? Susan was dead before I even met him."

"You said earlier that you knew Susan had drowned."

"Yes."

"When did you find out?"

Sandy shrugged. "I don't know. Several years ago, I guess. I don't exactly remember when."

"How did you find out?"

"Someone—someone told me. Why are you asking me all this? I tell you, I didn't leave you any note."

"I'm not accusing you of anything." Annie put her hand over Sandy's. "I just want to know what's going on, and why someone doesn't want me looking into Susan's past."

Sandy shrugged again, this time with a ghost of a smile.

"Maybe whoever it was didn't want you wasting your time on a memory."

Annie sighed. "You really can't tell me anything else about Susan?"

"I really can't." Sandy looked out over the backyard, and there was a little quaver in her voice. "But thank you for caring about her enough to try to find out more."

They were both silent for another moment and then Annie stood up.

"I'm sorry to have bothered you again. I'd still like us to be friends, though. I mean, if you ever feel like company."

Sandy stood, too, and walked with her toward the front of the house. "I'm sure we both have plenty to keep us busy. Anyway, I'm fine here on my own."

They were at the big oak now, and Annie gave it one last fond look.

"I've always liked this tree. Oaks are so reliable."

"They say this one was planted when they built the house," Sandy said, "so I guess it's pretty old."

Annie put her hand on one of the weathered strips of wood that had once been a ladder up into the tree limbs, and from what she remembered from her girlhood, nearly into the sky.

"I always loved playing up there."

Sandy looked up into the swaying branches. "Almost like playing in the clouds."

Annie looked at her, and Sandy's eyes widened. Then she laughed softly. "All kids pretend that, don't they?"

"The only one ever I knew was Susan," Annie said.

Sandy shrugged, still half smiling. "Then that's where I

must have gotten it from. That first time my dad brought me here, when she and I were very young."

Annie looked at her, studying her face, the nuances of her expression, the touch of uncertainty in her wide blue eyes. She couldn't possibly be—

"I have a lot to do." Sandy ducked her dark head. "Thanks for coming by, but I do need to go."

Before Annie could find her voice, Sandy had scurried into the house and shut the door.

Playing in the clouds.

Once again, Annie looked up into the tree and then toward the silent house.

"Susan?"

*   *   *   *

She had found her. She had found Susan.

Annie knew it now without a doubt, and without a doubt Susan knew that Annie knew. It was almost surreal to think that, all this time, Susan had lived right here in Stony Point, pretending to be Sandy Maxwell. And still she was pretending.

"Why?" Annie asked again, hardly seeing the road as she drove back to Grey Gables. "What are you hiding from? And what am I supposed to do next?"

As soon as she got home, she saw the light on her answering machine flashing. Absently, she pushed the button. "Hey, Annie, it's Alice. You won't believe who I saw in the Gas N Go a little while ago. Archer Prescott! I'm sure it was him. Call me."

Annie froze where she stood, her car keys still clutched in her hand. Archer Prescott was in Stony Point. Why would a man like Prescott come here?

Annie knew why. It wasn't a *what* that Susan was hiding from. It was a *who*.

She shook her head. If Susan didn't want to marry him, why hadn't she just left? Why the elaborate deception?

It didn't matter. Whatever her reasons, she wanted everyone, including Prescott, to think she was dead, and Annie had led him right to her. At the very least, she could let Susan know he was in town.

She got into her car and hurried back out to the old Morris house. It wasn't likely that Susan would appreciate what she had done, stirring up the past, bringing her back to whatever had made her want to disappear, but Annie couldn't let that stop her now. She had to talk to Susan, and she had to talk to her right away. If she was wrong about Prescott, then she was wrong. The worst that could happen is that Susan would order her off her property and tell her to never come back. But if Prescott *was* the one Susan was hiding from, the one she *had* been hiding from for almost twenty years …

Annie racked her brain as she walked up to the door, the question still haunting her. *Why? Why had Susan wanted to disappear? And why would Prescott still want to find her?*

Almost as soon as she knocked, the front door swung open. Susan stared at her, saying nothing, and her face was pale and blank. Had she been crying?

"I'm sorry to keep dropping in on you." Annie moved closer to the door, hoping she could have a few minutes with Susan before Prescott showed up. "I have something I need to tell you, and it can't wait. I hope I haven't ruined everything, but—"

"You'd better come in."

Susan stepped back into the house, and Annie crossed the threshold.

"Look, I know—"

The door clicked shut behind her, and she turned, startled to see a man standing there.

"I wasn't expecting to meet you here, Annie."

He was tall, and even in his 50s, lithe and powerfully built. His blond hair was salted with gray, especially at the temples, and his hands—

His hands were large, neatly groomed and manicured, the fingers circled with gold and jewels that spoke of wealth and status. Despite the smile on the man's face, those hands were somehow menacing. Perhaps it was their size and strength that frightened her. Perhaps it was that they held a wooden baseball bat.

"You're Archer Prescott."

She knew his voice from their telephone conversations. Even without that, she knew it was Prescott. She knew now what she had done.

She turned to Susan. "Sandy, I—"

"Uh, uh, uh." Prescott's smile grew slightly broader. "We ought to be honest with each other now, shouldn't we, Annie? You've already let the cat out of the bag anyway. I'd say it's time for some straight talk, isn't it, Susan?"

"Please." Susan cringed away from him, her voice hardly more than a whimper. "Please, please."

Annie went to her, sheltering her in her arms. "I'm so sorry. I didn't understand. I didn't know—"

Prescott gestured with the bat. "I think the two of you ought to sit down on the couch in there where I can keep an eye on you. Susan and I were about to have a nice little chat."

He grinned again, and the determined coolness in his china-blue eyes made Annie cling closer to her terrified friend.

Again, he gestured. "Go on, now. Before I see to things here, I have some questions I want answered. Things I've wondered about for a good number of years now. Things only my darling Susan can tell me."

Pulling Annie with her, Susan stumbled toward the little sitting room where the two of them had talked on Annie's first visit. The room was still warm and bright, and a welcoming fire crackled in the hearth, but Annie couldn't help feeling cold. Susan was trembling against her.

Prescott sneered at them both.

"That's some friend you have there, Susan. She was so eager to meddle in your business, she told me all about her research and meeting your 'Cousin Sandy.'"

Susan glanced at Annie and then dropped her eyes. There was bewildered hurt in those eyes, and beyond that, hopeless fear.

Annie squeezed both of her hands. "I didn't know. I didn't put it all together until just today. Why did you—?"

"You should have thought harder, Annie." Prescott slid one hand along the smooth wood of the bat. "I told you myself how long I searched for Susan after she supposedly drowned. I had teams of people looking, and they kept on looking for weeks afterward. Even years after that, I had people keeping their eyes open. Just in case. It's the kind of man I am. I know things, and what I don't know, I find out. I have people. Resources. I don't leave things to chance. When I first met Susan all those years ago, I had her checked out. Her family, her friends. I knew everything about her, and them. Did you think this 'Cousin Sandy' story was going to fool me?"

"Please," Susan begged. "Can't you just leave us all alone? I wasn't going to say anything. It's been twenty years now. If I was going to say anything, I would have already."

"You shouldn't have dyed your hair, Susan. Natural blondes are too hard to come by." Prescott shook his head. "You're still not bad to look at though, for your age and all, but not when you cry. I told you years ago, you shouldn't ever cry. It spoils your looks. But it doesn't much matter now, does it?"

He stepped back, leaning slightly so he could look out the front windows, obviously making sure no other unexpected company had shown up, and Susan made a slight sobbing noise.

"What did I tell you about spoiling your looks, Susan?"

Prescott tipped her chin up to him, and Susan shrank back, her eyes wide with fear. Her shaky breath was suddenly silent.

Annie steeled herself. "What do you want?"

A slow grin spread once again across Prescott's face. "Closure. Isn't that what everybody wants? I just want to make sure it's final this time." He still had one finger on Susan's chin, making her keep her eyes on him. "You didn't think you could really leave me, did you, darling? Nobody leaves Archer Prescott. Don't you remember?"

"Please, Archer. I had to. I couldn't stand it anymore."

He removed his hand, shoving Susan's head back as he did, and then he turned to Annie. "And you, Annie, you don't seem to know when to mind your own business. Now it's a little too late for turning back."

Annie straightened her shoulders, forcing herself to look him coolly in the eyes. "People know I was coming here. They know you were coming here. If anything happens to us, if you do anything at all, they'll know. You won't be able to just walk away." She paused, letting him think. "But it's not too late to do it now."

He laughed to himself, the same warm chuckle she had heard over the phone before, only now it made her blood run cold. "Sure they know. They'll know I came out here to talk to the lady who owns Susan's old house, the lady *you* told me about. They'll know you came out to talk to us both. And once I'm gone, they'll know you two were just fine when I left you. They'll even know that friendly Mrs. Dawson decided to accept 'Sandy's' invitation to stay to dinner so you two could get better acquainted. Now what could be nicer than that?"

"Her husband was on his way here when I left town," Annie bluffed. "He'll be at the door any minute now. If you go now, nobody has to even know you were here. I promise we won't say anything."

"No," Prescott agreed. "You won't say anything. And neither will her husband. I've already made sure of that."

Annie glanced at Susan. "Tom's here?"

"In the kitchen." Again tears sprang to Susan's eyes. "He came in the back door. Archer was already here with that bat—"

"You know what they say about weaving tangled webs, don't you, Susan? You shouldn't have tried to deceive me. You knew I'd find out. No matter how long it took."

"Please. Tom's hurt. Let me—"

"He's all right. And he won't have to last much longer anyway."

"What are you going to do?" Annie demanded.

"Once you mentioned 'Cousin Sandy' was living here in this house, I started thinking about what I should do. I couldn't leave my darling Susan out here with just good old Tom to keep her company. She might get bored and start talking too much."

Susan screwed her eyes shut and shook her head. "No. No, I won't. I promise. I swear!"

"Shh." Annie squeezed her arm around the other woman, trying to calm her. Then she glared at Prescott. "What are you going to do?"

"I remember this house very well from when I used to visit Susan here." Prescott looked thoughtful for a moment. "Houses like this, the really old ones, you've got to be careful with them. This one is heated with propane, and that can be deadly if you don't store the containers the right way."

Annie glanced at Susan, but she only looked bewildered.

"The tanks are out back where they should be. Tom's always careful—"

"You put a propane tank in a closed space, like that

basement down there," Prescott continued, "and if it leaks, there's no place for the gas to disperse. The propane itself isn't actually toxic, but you get down in a place where it's concentrated and there's not enough oxygen. You drown, just as if you were in twenty feet of water." He winked at Susan. "Or in the ocean a couple of miles off the Carolina coast."

"I couldn't stand it, Archer. You scared me, and I knew you'd never let me get away. That's all I wanted. I wasn't going to tell. You don't have to do this."

"It's too late now, my darling. Your friend here has a big mouth, and I'm sure, a righteous sense of civic duty. Even if you didn't say anything, she would. Better to settle this now and for good."

"How are you going to explain it?" Annie forced herself to be calm and logical. "Why would we all be down in the basement?"

"Good question, and I made sure I had an answer for it when I was figuring out what to do. Something I could be sure the police would think of all on their own. Something that would let them close the books on another unfortunate accident." Again he ran his hand along the side of the bat. "Everyone knows that if Mr. Homeowner suspects he has a propane leak, he'll naturally want to go down to the basement and check it out. When he doesn't come back upstairs after a while, of course Mrs. Homeowner is going to go check on him. That was going to be the end of it until you showed up, Annie. Now, of course, when *Sandy* sees her husband lying on the floor unconscious, knowing she can't get him back up by herself, she'll call her new friend to help her out. Sadly, the two ladies will also be overcome."

Annie looked him straight in the eye. "Do you think we're just going to go down there and wait to die?"

"That's where my little buddy here comes in." Prescott held the bat in both hands over his shoulder as if he were waiting for a pitch. "Tap somebody just right, not hard enough for a postmortem to find any skull fractures, and he becomes really cooperative. Like good old Tom out there in the kitchen."

"They may not find fractures," said Annie, "but they'll find bruising on all three of us. No coincidence could explain that. They'll know it wasn't an accident."

"Not by what's left after a house fire. Another reason it's not smart and not legal to store propane inside, especially in an old tinderbox like this. I remember that there's a hot water heater in that basement. When the flame eventually catches the propane gas, that's all it will take." Prescott took a moment to admire the bat. "And in the fire, Exhibit A here is reduced to ashes along with everything and everyone else. No weapon, no blood, no DNA, no fingerprints ... and no witnesses."

"They'll find you, you know. There's always something criminals don't account for, and the police figure it out every time."

"Not every time. Not if you're smart enough. Not if they're convinced there was no crime." His mouth turned up slightly at one side. "Not if there's nobody left to talk."

Stall for time. Annie knew that, as long as she could keep him talking, they'd have a chance to figure a way out of this. Maybe Tom would wake up out there in the kitchen and rescue them. Maybe the cavalry would come riding over the hill. Something. Anything. She just had to stall for time and pray. "You said you wanted to ask Susan about some things. Have you forgotten?"

"After twenty years? Not on your life." The grin reappeared. "No pun intended."

"You'd better ask her, then. While you have a chance. Before the police come for you."

"You know, Annie, I can't decide if you're a good bluffer or just stupid. Either way, we both know that's not happening. In a little nowhere like this? What, Deputy Fife is going to come put a headlock on me?"

Annie merely looked at him, hoping her expression was confident enough to make him wonder if she might be telling the truth.

"But she's right, darling Susan. I have some things I want to know. You know I don't like being outsmarted. If it happens, I want to know how it was done so I can keep it from happening again. So now you tell me how you managed to disappear like that. I wouldn't have thought a shrinking violet like you would have the backbone to do it."

"I just—" Susan took three or four quick breaths and then steadied herself. "I wasn't trying to hurt you, Archer. I didn't want to make you mad. You wanted—you wanted me to be somebody I couldn't be. I could never live up to everything you demanded in a girlfriend. I knew it would only get worse if I was your wife."

"Worse?" He shook his head, undisguised disbelief on his face. "I gave you everything. You never stepped outside without being covered in jewels, dressed in the latest fashions from New York and Paris. I gave you a European sports car. Once we were married, you would have had half a dozen mansions to live in, people to wait on you hand and foot, and whatever else you wanted day or night. That would have been worse?"

"I didn't want those things, Archer. I never wanted those things. You wanted those things for *you*, not for me. I had to wear certain clothes, drive a certain car, know certain people, look a certain way because that's what Archer Prescott's girlfriend was supposed to do. But you never listened to what Susan Morris wanted." A tear trickled out of the corner of Susan's eye. "What she needed."

Prescott snorted. "Don't give me that. You loved all that stuff. Every woman does. But I picked you. I picked you to be my wife, and you threw it all in my face."

"You didn't want a wife. You wanted a Barbie doll. You wanted something you could dress up and carry around with you to impress your friends."

"Why did you agree to marry me in the first place? If I was such a jerk, why did you say yes?"

Susan wiped her face with both hands. "I thought you loved me. I really thought you did. Everybody told me you must, the way you showered me with presents all the time. Every time you screamed at me and told me I was stupid, and it was a good thing I had you to take care of me, I thought somewhere inside, you must love me. I thought we'd work things out in time. I thought maybe you just didn't realize how I felt, and I was afraid if I told you I'd lose you too." She glanced at Annie, her eyes pleading for understanding. "But then I realized I couldn't dress perfect and act perfect and feel perfect all the time. I wasn't a fashion model, and I didn't want to always dress like one. I wasn't a high society girl. I couldn't play that forever. I wasn't what you wanted, and no matter how much you pushed me, I couldn't be what you wanted. And after that night on the boat, that night we were docked at Brockton—" Again she glanced at Annie. "Archer, I knew you'd never let me go. I had to do something."

"So how'd you pull it off?" He looked her up and down. "How in the world did you ever have the courage to pull it off?"

Susan swallowed hard and then straightened her shoulders, daring to look him in the eye. "I didn't sleep at all that night. I just kept thinking about what you said. 'Once we're married, nobody can ever make you testify against me.' I knew after that, you'd never let me go. I knew that, if I tried to leave, you'd just come after me. There was nothing else I could do."

Annie bit her lip. "But why—?"

"Why didn't I tell someone? Why didn't I get help? I had no family anymore. No real friends. Nobody to look after me anymore. You've obviously never been around someone with his kind of money, with his connections. Make the wrong man mad, and you end up in a 'rest home' for people with mental issues or a 'treatment center' for those with a tragic addiction to pain medication. Or maybe you *accidentally* overdose on some designer drug that happens to be popular at the time, something he'd been begging you to get treatment for for months and months. Or maybe you just disappear." She glanced at Archer. "Wasn't that how you explained it to me in Brockton?"

He looked her up and down, blatant contempt on his

face. "You never were very smart, you know. You probably would have made me do something like that, in time."

"I guess I decided I'd rather disappear on my terms than yours."

"I still want to know how you did it. You had no money. No friends."

"Yes, you made sure of that. But you forgot the jewelry. Those diamond solitaire earrings and the matching bracelet, the ones I was wearing when I left the boat, were fakes. While you were having lunch with that stock trader in Brentwood, I pawned the real ones, bought some cheap replacements, and hid the money. You had told me not to leave the boat, and usually I was scared enough that I didn't. That day, I was too scared not to. I had just gotten back aboard when you showed up. I remember thinking you could hear my heart pounding and being sure you knew where I had been."

"So you were a deceitful little thief as well as an ingrate. I don't know why I ever tried to make something out of a piece of trash like you."

She licked her trembling lips. "Later on, when I knew a storm was coming up, I decided it was time to do what I had planned. Did you ever wonder why you slept the whole night that night? I put some of my sleeping pills in your coffee. Not so many that you'd really notice, but enough to keep you under until I had gotten away. I was always a good swimmer, remember, Annie?"

Annie nodded, and Susan turned again to Prescott.

"Once I was sure you were asleep, I put the boat in toward the coast a bit. When we were about two miles out, I turned it back toward open water and slipped over the side. I had made myself a little packet of clothes and shoes that I put in a waterproof bag I had also gotten at the pawnshop. When I got to shore, I made sure I came up on some rocks so I wouldn't leave any footprints in the sand. I hid there and rested for a while. Then I went up into the trees and changed into my dry clothes and cut my hair short. I caught a bus that took me into Charleston, and from there, I got the night bus to Atlanta.

"The next day, I had my hair fixed. The salon was one of those cheap places you would have never even heard of. Cut and color cost 25 dollars. I took a few more bus rides after that. Every time I stopped, I changed something about myself. Just some little something that would make me blend in and keep anyone from tying me to you. I earned a little money here and there waiting tables or washing dishes. I spent a few nights in women's shelters and in a couple of churches where they didn't ask questions.

"I told people I was Sandy Childress, and nobody ever questioned it. I didn't drive or vote or buy on credit, so I never needed proof of my identity. Then, after I married Tom, I was Mrs. Maxwell, and he took care of everything else. Susan Morris really was gone."

Annie tried to imagine the courage that must have required. "Then Tom knew about you."

Susan nodded, and her calmness crumbled into tears. "Always. I met him in El Dorado, and he was so down-to-earth, and so easy to talk to. It took me a while to trust him, but I never regretted it. He made me feel like I was worth something just the way I was."

Prescott sneered. "Well, isn't that just sweet. And in return, you get him his head knocked in."

Susan started to sob, and his sneer deepened into a scowl.

"Stop crying. You make me sick."

"Why can't you just leave us alone?" she wailed. "He never did anything to you! He never hurt anybody!"

"I told you to stop crying!" His face was transformed into an ugly mask of rage. "It's not going to help! It never helps! It makes you weak, and it makes you ugly! I don't need ugly people around me!"

She froze, her eyes fixed on him, her body seeming to shrink into itself as he loomed over her. She didn't make a sound. Didn't breathe. Didn't dare.

Annie wanted to shrink back too. No matter what it was that Susan knew and had not told anyone all these years, whatever it was she had found out while she and Prescott were in Brockton, it was obvious why she had wanted to escape this man.

Just then, the phone in Annie's purse started chirping. All three of them stared at it until it stopped. Then it immediately started ringing again.

"I told you people are looking for me."

Annie's voice was low and controlled, and for a moment Prescott only glared at her. Then he snatched the phone out of the bag and threw it into the cracking fire, grinning as the ringing abruptly stopped.

"I guess your number is now unavailable."

Still holding Susan's hand, Annie stood up, channeling her fear into indignation.

"Well, you're a fine bully, aren't you? Good at pushing

people around? Are you proud of having badgered a twenty-two-year-old girl into faking her own death just to escape you?"

He turned on her. "Sit down and shut up about things you don't know."

Annie squeezed Susan's hand, not taking her eyes off him.

"No matter what happens to us, it won't change anything for you. Look at her. She's terrified of you. Is that what you want? You can't get people to love you, so you have to use your money and your power to bribe and bully and force them to do what you tell them?"

"I said shut up!"

"Is your wife terrified of you too? Does she cringe every time you get close to her?"

"Shut up! Shut up!"

He lifted the bat, ready to swing it, and Annie flung herself at him, wrapping her arms around him so he had no leverage. He tried to shove her off, but she clung to him.

"Help me! Susan, help me!"

Forced to drop the bat, Prescott was cursing at her, trying to throw her to the floor, but still she clung to him.

"Susan! You've got to help me!"

Susan sat frozen there, her eyes wide, her lips quivering. Then with a low cry, she leaped to her feet and grabbed the bat.

"Let her go, Archer." Her voice was low and fierce, her eyes steely. Here at last was the woman who had somehow found the courage to break free from Prescott before. "Let her go, or God forgive me, I'll use this."

Prescott studied her for an eternity of a moment, and

Annie loosened her grip. She began to back away from him, but without warning, he seized her arm, holding her in front of him, between him and Susan.

"Looks like we have a bit of a standoff now. What are you going to do?"

"I'm going to get that phone over there and call the police. And if you move, I'll use the bat. I promise I will," Susan said.

Annie gasped as Prescott's hand snaked around her throat.

"And then what, darling Susan?" His voice was mocking, taunting. "Are you going to hit her to try to get to me? Put the bat down."

There was a flicker of uncertainty in Susan's eyes. "No. You let her go."

"I'm not going to tell you again, Susan. Don't make me do something you won't like." Prescott's strong fingers tightened on Annie's throat, and she squirmed against him.

"The phone," she gasped. "Get it."

"Don't do it, Susan." Prescott stepped forward, dragging Annie with him. "Give me the bat before I get angry. You used to always make me angry, even when I wanted to be nice to you. Don't make that mistake again."

Susan made a little whimpering noise, and the bat she held trembled.

"Susan, don't—" The pressure on Annie's throat increased, cutting her off. She struggled to pull Prescott's hand away, to free herself, but she wasn't strong enough.

"Now, Susan. Give it to me. Don't make me—" Abruptly, he shoved Annie toward Susan, throwing them both onto the couch. An instant later, he had snatched up the baseball bat and was standing over them with it.

"We're done now, and I have a plane to catch. Say good-bye."

~ 17 ~

Susan covered her face and ducked her head against Annie's shoulder. Annie's eyes were fixed on the bat as Prescott swung it over his shoulder, the muscles in his arms flexing, ready to bring it down on them.

"Dear God," she breathed. "Please—"

"Mrs. Maxwell? Mrs. Maxwell? Are you all right? This is the police! Open the door!" Strong blows on the front door echoed through the house. "Open up!"

"We're in here!" Annie screamed. "We're in here!"

With an animal roar, Prescott flung the bat toward the front door and then bolted down the hallway.

Annie leaped up from the couch, ran to the door, and threw it open.

"He ran out the back! Hurry!"

Chief Edwards gestured to the fresh-faced young officer he'd brought with him. "Don't let him make it into the woods, Peters. I'll go around the other way."

With a glance at Annie, Peters clattered through the house and out the back door after Prescott.

Chief Edwards took Annie's arm. "Are you ladies all right?"

Annie could only shake her head breathlessly, not knowing whether to laugh or cry. Susan was definitely crying.

"My husband's hurt. Get an ambulance. Please."

She and Annie hurried into the kitchen. Chief Edwards followed them, using his cell phone to request medical help and backup from the county police. Then he stormed out the back door after Prescott.

Tom was sprawled face-down on the kitchen floor, a trickle of drying blood coming from above his right eye. Annie noticed the corresponding smear on the corner of the tiled countertop, and she quickly felt for a pulse in Tom's neck. "He must've hit his head on the way down, but he's alive."

Susan sank to her knees beside him.

"Better not move him. Let the paramedics check him out first." Annie glanced out the window toward the woods, wondering why Chief Edwards' shouted commands had suddenly ceased. Then she turned back to Susan. "You don't want to make any head or neck injury worse."

Susan nodded. She touched her fingers to her husband's hair, murmuring his name as tears slipped down her cheeks.

Annie knelt beside her, glad to see that Tom was breathing regularly despite his unconsciousness. There was a trail of blood from the back of his head down to a corresponding stain on his shirt collar.

The police chief came back inside, studied Tom for a moment, and then looked at Susan. "So this is Tom Maxwell?"

"Yes, of course."

"We thought that was who we were chasing out there."

Annie's forehead wrinkled. "Really?"

"Ms. Brock from the yarn store called us up and said Maxwell was heading out here to make trouble for you and for his wife, and that we'd better get out here quick.

What's going on? Is the man we caught the Prescott you told me about?"

"Yes."

"JFP Athletics?"

Annie nodded. "It's a long story, but he was planning on killing all three of us."

Chief Edwards whistled low. "Mr. Prescott's going to have some explaining to do. He didn't hurt either of you, did he?"

"He didn't get the chance to," Annie reported, catching Susan's eye.

Susan covered her face with both hands and then used them to wipe her tears. "Annie. Oh, Annie, after all these years, what have you done?"

Annie shook her head helplessly. "I'm so sorry, Susan. I had no idea something like this would happen. I just wanted to—"

They all turned when the back door opened.

"Chief, our perp's packed up and ready to go." Officer Peters grinned, his breath gradually slowing.

"Good work. We didn't exactly have time for introductions, Mrs. Dawson, but this is Cal Peters. I borrowed him from the county police to take Roy's place. We might even see about a permanent transfer."

Annie merely lifted one eyebrow and then smiled at the young man. "It's good to meet you, Cal. Especially now. Thanks for catching—"

Cal's face turned a little pink. "It wasn't anything, ma'am. I just ran him down over by the little graveyard back there, cuffed him, and put him in the car."

Chief Edwards nodded. "Good job too."

"Did he say anything?" Annie asked.

"Nothing but 'I want my lawyer.'" The young officer glanced down at Tom Maxwell. "I went ahead and charged Prescott with assault, Chief. Anything else?"

"That'll do for now, though I have the feeling we'll have quite a list of charges once I get a chance to talk to these ladies."

The wail of sirens cut through the air, piercing Tom's unconsciousness. He groaned as he tried to lift his head. "Susan?"

She smoothed back the hair that had fallen over his forehead and slipped her other hand under his cheek. "Don't get up, Tommy. The ambulance is here. They'll take care of you."

"That man—"

"Shh, it's all right. Just relax. Everything's OK."

He closed his eyes and let out a slow breath. "If you say so."

Soon the medics had him on a gurney and then in the ambulance. Susan and Annie walked out to the driveway after them.

"Do you think you could drive me to the hospital?" There was a lopsided grin on Susan's tear-stained face. "I haven't had a driver's license in decades."

"Of course. Anything you need."

The ambulance pulled away, revealing the Stony Point Police car and another from Lincoln County, their red and blue lights still flashing. In the back of the county car sat Archer Prescott, head down, face sullen. Just then he turned their way.

He fixed his eyes on Susan and then on Annie, darkly, deliberately, and then gave a little nod. There was no more than that, but it was an obvious threat.

Annie turned Susan away from him, back toward the house. "I'm so sorry about all this. I never dreamed it would turn out this way." She realized that Susan was crying again, and she put her arms around her.

"Mrs. Maxwell?"

Susan lifted her head and blotted her face with her sleeve. "Chief Edwards. I never did thank you for coming. I don't know what we would have done—"

"I'm glad we were in time, ma'am. We're going to see that Mr. Prescott is taken care of, so you don't need to worry about that. He'll be spending some time with our friends at the county jail; then I wouldn't be surprised if he spends quite a long while after that in one of the state facilities. You will both need to give me statements about everything that's happened here."

Susan glanced at Annie. "We were going to the hospital."

"That's fine," the chief assured her. "You'll want to check on your husband. As soon as possible, we'll need to get all the details sorted out."

Annie looked over at the police car and saw that Prescott's head was down again. He was probably working on some way to explain away everything he had done. Some way to bully or bribe his way out of the trouble he was in.

"Don't you worry about him anymore, ma'am. There's only so much that money can buy, especially once everything is out in the open." Chief Edwards touched two fingers to the brim of his hat.

"Let me get my purse, and we'll drive out to the hospital," Annie said.

She turned to go back into the house, but Susan grabbed her hand.

"Annie." She swallowed hard, and once again her eyes brimmed with tears. "Annie, I—"

"He's going to be all right. The paramedics don't think there's any permanent damage."

Susan shook her head. "I was so scared. It was as if twenty years hadn't happened and I was still a scared little girl afraid to breathe if I thought it would make Archer mad."

"But you didn't let that stop you from doing what you had to do—not then and not now. I know you were scared." Annie twisted her keys in her hand. "I was pretty terrified myself. But we didn't let him bully us, did we?"

"No." The realization brought a half smile to Susan's lips. "No, we didn't."

"Now, come on. Your husband is going to be wondering where you are."

~ 18 ~

"*I*t was so easy."

Susan stared straight ahead, watching the road vanish under them. Annie hadn't wanted to trouble her with questions as they drove to the hospital, but Susan seemed relieved to finally be able to tell her everything.

"It was easy to fall into the trap. I had been in some shows, on and off Broadway, and I had decided I really didn't want to continue. It's a hard business, and if you want to stay in it for long, you have to make compromises, especially if you're a young girl. I didn't want to make those compromises, so I was thinking of giving it all up."

"And then you met Archer Prescott."

"Yeah." Susan sighed. "At first he was unbelievably wonderful. He was funny and kind and generous—amazingly generous. All I had to do was admire something I saw in a store window, and he'd get it for me. He gave me clothes and jewelry, anything and everything. And he was so attentive. He would call me two or three times a day just to tell me he was crazy about me, or that he thought I was beautiful, or that we should get married. How could I help being flattered?"

"Who wouldn't be?"

"But it was too much, and it was too soon. He wanted me to spend every minute with him. He'd get upset if I wanted to do something without him or just hang out with my friends. Aunt Kim said I didn't seem happy anymore, and she was right. It was too stressful always going to some society function and worrying about looking just right. Sometimes I wanted to be able to go to the corner store just in jeans and a sweatshirt, or wear flats instead of spike heels, you know?"

"Archer didn't like that?"

"No. I remember the first real fight we had. It was over my shoes. I'm surprised the people in the next apartment didn't call the police on us the way he screamed and cursed and threw things at me. I stayed home and cried for two days after that, and planned to never see him again."

"Obviously, you did though. Why?"

"He sent me flowers and left me messages and begged me to let him explain. I finally called him, and he cried on the phone. He told me he was so sorry. He said his father had always yelled at him when he was a little boy, and sometimes it was hard for him to not do the same thing when he was upset. And he told me about some things that had been going on at his company that he was worried about, things that he had taken out on me. I couldn't help feeling sorry for him, and I told him I'd see him again."

Annie merely raised one eyebrow, and Susan ducked her head.

"I know. I know. I should have never let him treat me that way, not even once. But I wanted to be kind. I wanted to understand what he was going through and help him get past it. But when it happened again and again, I decided I had enough. When Aunt Kim died, I broke things off with him and came back home to Stony Point. He'd send me roses from time to time or leave messages on the answering machine, but I forced myself to ignore them. Then, right after my parents died, he called. He had sent flowers to the funeral and the sweetest card. I needed—" Susan's voice broke. "I needed somebody. He told me again how sorry he was about the way things had ended between us. He said he knew we belonged together, and he promised to make me happy. I needed to be happy."

"So you told him you'd marry him."

"It was OK for a while. I didn't want to think. I didn't want to make even the smallest decisions for myself. I guess I was deep in depression, I don't know. He liked it that way, though. I just did what he wanted, and I did it all the time. But after a while, I started coming out of it. I started having my own opinions and my own plans. I tried to break it off with him. I even canceled the plans he had made for us to be married in Stony Point."

"Reverend Wallace said it was because you wanted a big wedding out of state."

"Archer must have told him that. All I said was that I hadn't decided exactly what I wanted to do. Poor Reverend Wallace. He was so nice to me."

"Why didn't you talk to him?" Annie asked. "Why didn't you tell him what you were going through? He could have helped you or gotten you the help you needed."

"I was so wrapped up in grief that I couldn't deal with people. And after a while, Archer had me so beaten down, I didn't think I could function on my own. I wanted out, but he had convinced me that I couldn't make it without him."

Annie was silent for a moment, waiting for Susan to

continue, but she didn't. Finally, while they waited at a stoplight, Annie turned to her.

"What happened in Brockton?"

There was something cynical in Susan's low laugh. "You'd think after knowing Archer as long as I did, it wouldn't have bothered me. I had put up with his tirades and his insults and his demands before. That time was different. I knew before I even said anything that he was going to be mad. I just hadn't realized how bad it would be."

"What did you say?"

Susan took a deep breath. "I shouldn't have said anything—not that night of all nights. He had agreed to meet his brother Donny at some club in Brockton, just to talk things out, he said. I don't know why he even went. They always fought when they got together. They couldn't even talk on the phone and be civil to each other, at least Archer couldn't. Anyway, Archer didn't usually drink more than he could handle, but anytime he and one of his brothers fought, his drinking got out of control. And when he drank, he talked too much. I asked him how much he'd had, and he cursed at me and told me to stay out of his business. That was when I told him maybe we should take a break."

"And—?"

"That was it. I didn't break off the engagement. I didn't tell him I never wanted to see him again. I just told him we should think about taking a break." Her breathing quickened at the memory. "I thought he was going to kill me right there. He said if I ever tried to leave, he'd make me sorry. He told me all those horrible ways he knew to get rid of someone and make it look as if he didn't have anything to do with it. I don't know how, but I managed to stand up to him a little bit. I told him it was all talk, that he wouldn't dare really do something like that to me or anyone." She swallowed hard. "That only made him laugh. That nasty laugh he has when he knows you're helpless."

Annie nodded. It was enough to have dealt with that just once. How in the world had Susan been able to bear it all those months when she was with him?

Susan took another shaky breath. "He said he would do anything to get what he wanted. And to prove it, he told me why he had inherited the company and didn't have to share it with his brothers. He had forged his father's will."

Annie could only stare at her. "What? He stole everything from his own family? That huge company? All that money?"

"Yes. And the next day, when he was sober and realized what he had said, he told me we'd have to get married so I couldn't be forced to testify against him. He said it as if it was just a joke, but I knew then that I had to do something, and I had to do it quickly. He told me he was sorry for what had happened and that he would make it up to me. I let him think that I was OK with it, that like everything else he had done, it didn't bother me. But I knew I had to go."

The car behind them tapped its horn, and seeing the light had changed, Annie took her foot off the brake and pulled into the intersection.

"But the will. Nobody ever questioned it?"

"He was pretty smart about it. He didn't cut his brothers out entirely. That would have caused too much suspicion. They still ended up with a lot of money and some of the other properties, but he got JFP Athletics all to himself. He had switched out the page in the will that mentioned the disposition of the property. All of the other pages, including the ones signed by the witnesses and notary, were originals. So if the will had been contested in court, all of those people could honestly swear they had seen Jason Prescott sign his will. There was even the appropriate notation in the notary's register book, all perfectly legal and above board."

"But wouldn't the witnesses know what was in the will they saw Jason sign?"

Susan shook her head. "He told me they had witnessed the signature, but the contents of the will were kept private. Only the lawyer who had drawn it up would have known, and he was dead."

"But wouldn't the paper and the ink be different on that page? And the machine it was printed on?"

"I don't know. I guess the police will do some digging once this all comes out."

"It *is* going to come out, right?" Annie glanced at her and then turned her eyes back to the road. "You've got to tell them now, Susan."

Susan nodded. "I should have done it a long time ago. I've wasted twenty years of my life being afraid of a man who's really no more than a coward and a bully."

"I hope it wasn't all a waste."

"No." There was a sudden glow in Susan's weary eyes. "Tom was never a waste. He took me just the way I was, no questions asked. I know he sounded rude to you, but he's really not like that. He just knew how scared I was and tried his best to protect me."

"It makes more sense to me now."

"He always wanted me to stand up to Archer, but he never tried to push me to do anything. Now that it's all over, I'm sorry I didn't listen to him in the first place. And I'm sorry he's the one who's had to get hurt by a decision I made."

Annie took her eyes off the road just long enough make sure Susan was looking at her.

"It wasn't your decision, and it wasn't my decision. I've been blaming myself for stirring up all this, for bringing Prescott here. But he was the one who made the wrong decisions. He was the one who's been hurting other people—not me and not you." She reached over and squeezed Susan's hand. "And you're going to be with Tom in just a few minutes. I'm sure that's the best medicine he could have."

By then they were at the county hospital, and the two of them hurried inside.

*   *   *   *

Annie drove back to Stony Point alone. She had offered to stay at the hospital, but Susan said she was fine there with Tom. She had permission to stay in his room with him overnight, and they were both expected to be able to come home the next day. Annie had volunteered to drive them home again then, and Susan had gratefully accepted.

For now, Annie was just happy to see Grey Gables come into view. Poor Boots must be half starved, and Annie could think of nothing more inviting than a hot bath and her own soft bed. When she pulled into the drive, though, she realized she wasn't going to get either for a little while yet.

Alice and Mary Beth had obviously spotted her car from the carriage house and were hurrying over to her.

"Annie, are you all right?" Alice opened the driver's side door and practically pulled Annie to her feet. "We were so worried."

Mary Beth wrapped Annie in a motherly hug. "I knew we were going to have trouble as soon as I realized Tom Maxwell wasn't in the basement anymore. I tried forever to call you, and just kept getting a message that said your number was unavailable."

"Come over and have some coffee with us," Alice said. "I know you must be worn out, but you've got to tell us what happened."

Annie took each of the others by one arm. "You both come have coffee with me. I need to feed Boots, and if I don't get out of these shoes pretty soon I'm going to keel over."

Soon the three of them were sitting at the big table in the kitchen. Boots had quickly lost interest in the food Annie put down for her and was content to lie with her head resting on Annie's feet. Annie smiled wearily, soothed by her rumbling purr.

"I didn't even know he was gone." Mary Beth warmed her hands on the generous mug of coffee in front of her. "I had several customers after Alice came in, and it wasn't until I went down to get some needles from a new shipment that I realized he wasn't there anymore. He must have heard us mention Prescott's name and that he was in town."

Annie turned to Alice. "And you saw Prescott at the Gas N Go?"

"You know how Scooter always runs your credit card and then thanks you by name? I had just filled up, and I heard him say, 'Thank you, Mr. Prescott.' And I looked, and I just knew this guy looked like the picture on the JFP website. So I left you a message, and then I told Mary Beth about it when I went into the shop later on."

"I didn't think anything of it," Mary Beth said. "I thought that, if it was the same guy, you probably knew he was coming into town already. And we thought maybe he'd go talk to Sandy Maxwell, since she was living in Susan's old house."

"Then why'd you call the police?"

"I figured Tom might go out to the house if he thought Prescott was going to try to talk to his wife. And I was afraid, after the last time, that Tom might cause trouble if he found you out there, too, so when I couldn't get you on the phone, I called the police."

"Good thing you did," Annie said. "You sent them after the wrong guy, but at least you sent them."

"Ian told us a little bit about what happened, but not much." Alice's eyes were wide. "I couldn't believe a man like Archer Prescott would really try to kill somebody—especially you."

"How did Ian find out?"

"He was in Chief Edwards' office when Mary Beth called. Ian made him promise to keep him posted on what was going on out there. He said he tried to call you too."

Mary Beth stirred a little more sugar into her coffee.

"So why didn't you answer your phone? I wanted to warn you that Tom was on his way there."

"I'm afraid my phone had a little bit of an accident. It ended up in the fireplace." Mary Beth made an exasperated little huff, and Annie chuckled. "Evidently the ringing was interrupting his talk with Susan."

"Susan?" Alice and Mary Beth both said it at once. Then Alice caught her breath. "Sandy Maxwell. Of course. It had to be!"

"Once I realized she was Susan I couldn't imagine why she would disappear the way she did, and why she didn't just walk away from him—Prescott—after she found out what kind of man he was. You know, Stella had sniffed him out. Then I saw him in action." Annie swallowed hard. "It got pretty scary there for a while."

"I can imagine." Mary Beth squeezed her hand. "Poor Annie."

"But, thank God and the people who were looking out for me, it turned out all right."

*   *   *   *

Even though she had objected to the idea at first, Annie was glad that Alice and Mary Beth had insisted on staying over that night. With Mary Beth in the guest room and Alice on the couch in the living room, Annie had spent a peacefully dreamless night. By midmorning, she was ready to give Chief Edwards all the details about her run-in with Archer Prescott.

"We talked with Mrs. Maxwell at the hospital, and

they've already analyzed the signatures on Prescott's father's will." Edwards glanced at the reports spread across his desk. "All legit except for the page that lists the bequests. It's a pretty good forgery. Close enough that nobody would think to check. Other than that, it's perfect."

"How'd he do that? Wouldn't the paper or the ink or something like that be different on the forged page?"

"That was the beauty of the plan. When his father mentioned that he had drawn up a new will, Archer got some of the same paper and the same pen his father had signed with so the forged page would match. Since it was one of the JFP attorneys who had made up the will, it was easy for Archer to slip in after hours and use the same computer to print out the new page."

"But wouldn't someone notice the difference in the computer file?"

"He changed it back. It wasn't until his father passed away that he changed the computer file permanently and switched out the page in the will in the hard copy. Nobody but the attorney and Mr. Prescott would have really known what was in the original, and the attorney had died a couple of years before the father. Archer even switched out the page in the unsigned copy of the will kept in the attorney's file so everything would match and nobody would know the difference. Then, when the will was probated, there was nothing anyone could question."

"That's a pretty heinous thing to do to your own family."

Edwards nodded. "And after all these years, I guess he felt like it was worth a few lives to protect himself. I've seen a lot of guys like that, and they only get worse over time. After a while, they start to think nothing is as important as what they want."

"I can't imagine being that greedy."

"It's not greed so much as narcissism. They start believing they deserve to have any and everything, no matter who it hurts."

Annie sighed and leaned back in her chair. "I'm just glad it's all over."

"We still have a few loose ends to tie up, but yeah, it is. Though, if you don't mind, Mrs. Dawson, someone else would like a word with you before you go."

Annie nodded. She didn't have to ask him who that someone else would be.

Chief Edwards pressed the button on his intercom. "Come on in."

Roy came through the door from his old office. He was dressed in civilian clothes, jeans and a button-down shirt, and carrying a packing box. He managed a hint of his habitual grin, but there was undeniable regret in it now.

"Hi, Annie. Can I talk to you alone for just a minute?"

He glanced at Chief Edwards, who looked to Annie.

"It's your decision, Mrs. Dawson. You don't have to if you don't want to. Officer Hamilton has officially tendered his resignation."

Annie looked at Roy. Something in his eyes pled for just this tiniest of concessions.

She turned back to the chief. "No, it's all right. I guess we both have a couple of things to say."

Edwards gave her a nod. "I'll be in the other room if you need me."

Roy waited until the door clicked shut; then he nodded toward the box in his arms. "Didn't have time enough to squirrel away much at this stop. I suppose, considering everything, that turned out for the best." He ducked his head. "I'm sorry for how I went about things, Annie, but I'm not sorry for the way I felt about you."

"Roy—"

"No, don't worry. I'm letting it go. I don't want you to think I'll be bothering you someday down the road. And believe you me, I won't ever be trying this kind of stunt anywhere ever again. But thank you for giving me a chance to start fresh and not have this on my permanent record."

Annie let her expression soften. "I didn't want you to lose your career, Roy; not over something you and I both know was just a stupid mistake."

He shrugged. "Sometimes love'll make you a little bit stupid."

He grinned suddenly, and Annie couldn't help a little smile of her own.

"You'll find the right girl one of these days. You're not a bad guy, you know? Just don't try to push things. When it's right, both of you will know."

"That's what they say." He didn't look entirely convinced, but he managed still to smile as he shifted his box against his hip and held out his hand. "Wish me luck?"

"Sure." She took his hand. "All the best, Roy."

"You're a nice lady, Annie. I doubt there's anybody out there like you, but if there is, I hope I find her."

He pressed her hand one last time and then released it. A moment later, he was gone.

Annie thought about him as she drove home, and she couldn't help but feel sorry for him. Still, she said a little prayer that he might one day find what he was looking for.

*   *   *   *

When she pulled up in front of Grey Gables, Annie saw she had a visitor.

"Susan!" She hurried up to the front porch. "How wonderful to see you. How did you get here?"

"I asked Chief Edwards if Cal Peters could drive me here after I finished giving my formal statement. I hope you don't mind me dropping in like this." Susan smiled shyly. "Turnabout's fair play and all."

"Of course it is. Come in. How's Tom today?"

"He's doing well. Really well. And so am I." Susan looked around the foyer. "I remember this house so well." She took a deep breath, and a little half smile softened her face. "It even smells the way it used to."

"I have some blueberry muffins. Would you join me?"

"I'd love to."

They went into the kitchen, and Annie pulled out a chair for her visitor. "Sit down, and I'll get us some coffee too."

"I always enjoyed coming to visit here, and your grandmother always made me feel so welcome."

"She loved having you over. I'm just sorry she never made a crocheter out of you."

"I never did finish that afghan, you know. I guess, left

to my own devices, I'm more of a gardener than a crafter, as much as I admired all the beautiful things she created."

"Gardening is an art in itself, if you ask me. But I don't think Gram would have minded your not learning to crochet—not nearly as much as she would have minded that you didn't come to her after your parents died."

"I know. After you told me she had passed away, I started thinking about her. I know she would have helped me. Archer had me so confused and scared, I didn't know what to do."

"Why did you even come back here? He would never have been able to trace you after all this time if you hadn't been living in your old house."

"I was raised in that house. It had been in my family since it was built. My family is buried out behind it. Why shouldn't my husband and I live in it?" She sighed. "I know, it was a risk. But I thought it would be all right after Archer moved the company out to the West Coast. Why would he even be looking for me after so much time had passed? And if he was, he wouldn't think I'd come back here, right? Tom called it hiding in plain sight, though I guess we weren't all that good at it."

"You managed to disappear for twenty years, so I guess you knew what you were doing. Oh, and by the way, that was sure some story you came up with ... the one about your grandfather and his two families. I could never have thought that up so quickly."

Susan's face colored. "Actually, Tom and I had invented that story, oh, I don't know how many years ago. He had said I should go ahead and make friends and get involved with people in town. Then, if anybody pried into my business, I could explain things that way. But I was too scared. I just wanted to stay at home and keep out of sight."

"Tom must really love you to try to protect your secret all that time."

"Oh." Susan bit her lip, and there was a hint of a smile in her eyes. "He wanted me to apologize to you for him."

"Apologize?"

"He's the one who sent you that first note. I didn't know he'd done it until he told me in the hospital. He said he felt kind of stupid doing it in the first place, but he was just trying to protect me."

Annie smiled. "I know."

Susan returned her smile, her blue eyes almost dreamily serene as she looked out over the ocean. "Do you know what? Besides being scared, I was really mad at you when Archer showed up at my house. I was mad at you for snooping around and bringing everything up again when I thought it had all been safely buried twenty years ago."

"Susan—"

"No, let me finish. I guess I had lived so long being afraid of him, always thinking I had to hide, I didn't realize how much I wanted to finally be free again. But you—" Tears sprang to her eyes. "You cared enough about a little girl you once knew to find out what had happened to her. And then, no matter how often I told you to go away, you cared enough about a stranger to make sure that she was all right. And even though he used it to try to hurt us both, you talked to Archer because you cared about him too. I always prayed that something could happen that would set me and

Tom free. Now I can see that even the painful things were all part of the answer."

Annie nodded. She had prayed, too, for Susan and for Sandy … and even for Archer Prescott. Susan was right, and her own missteps had all been part of a grand scheme to unlock that prison of fear.

"You know what else?" Susan ran her fingers through her short dark hair. "I believe I'll let my hair grow out. Even if there's a little gray in there now, I think it's time I was a blonde again."

She laughed, and her laugh brought Annie back to those days on the beach when two little girls built sand castles and played in the surf and learned they weren't such outsiders after all. She seemed so different from the frightened woman from a few weeks ago, and Annie knew why. She had found the Susan she had been searching for.

"Come on, Susan," she said with a smile. "Let's enjoy these muffins and catch up on the past twenty years."

Learn more about Annie's fiction books at

AnniesFiction.com

- Access your e-books
- Discover exciting new series
- Read sample chapters
- Watch video book trailers
- Share your feedback

We've designed the Annie's Fiction website especially for you!

Plus, manage your account online!

- Check your account status
- Make payments online
- Update your address

ANNIE'S ATTIC
MYSTERIES®

CREATIVE WOMAN
MYSTERIES®

Annie's
Quilted
Mysteries™

Annie's
Mysteries
Unraveled™